The Great Grown-Up Game of Make-Believe

STORIES

The Great Grown-Up Game of Make-Believe

STORIES

WINNER OF THE 2024 AUTUMN HOUSE FICTION PRIZE

Lauren D. Woods

AUTUMN HOUSE PRESS
Pittsburgh, PA

The Great Grown-Up Game of Make-Believe
Copyright © 2025 by Lauren D. Woods
Published by Autumn House Press
All Rights Reserved
ISBN: 978-1-63768-109-1

Cover & Interior Design: Kinsley Stocum
Cover Art Sources: Giersing, Harald. *Sovende pige.* 1910-1914, Watercolour Drawing.
Robinson, William Heath. *Then She Saw The Storks.* 1913, Illustration.
Author Photo: Nicole Harkin

LIBRARY OF CONGRESS CATALOGING-IN-PUBLICATION DATA
Names: Woods, Lauren D. author
Title: The great grown-up game of make-believe : stories / Lauren D. Woods.
Description: Pittsburgh, PA : Autumn House Press, 2025.
Identifiers: LCCN 2025013041 (print) | LCCN 2025013042 (ebook) |
ISBN 9781637681091 paperback | ISBN 9781637681145 epub
Subjects: LCGFT: Short stories
Classification: LCC PS3623.O676456 G74 2025 (print) | LCC PS3623.O676456 (ebook) |
DDC 813/.6--dc23/eng/20250530
LC record available at https://lccn.loc.gov/2025013041
LC ebook record available at https://lccn.loc.gov/2025013042

Printed in the United States on acid-free paper that meets the international standards of permanent books intended for purchase by libraries.

This is a work of fiction. All characters, events, and places described in this book are products of the author's imagination and are not intended to represent real persons, living or dead, or actual events.

Autumn House Press is a nonprofit corporation whose mission is the publication and promotion of poetry and other fine literature. The press gratefully acknowledges support from individual donors, public and private foundations, and government agencies. This book was supported, in part, by the Greater Pittsburgh Arts Council and the Pennsylvania Council on the Arts, a state agency funded by the Commonwealth of Pennsylvania.

For my parents, from whom I get my optimism

Table of Contents

The Great Grown-Up Game of Make-Believe

The Shape-Shifter

The shape-shifter met her husband during her horse era. She: gleaming and muscular, with a chestnut coat and black mane. He: heart pounding, face sweating. A few weeks into their time together, he licked his lips and said there must be no one like her in all the world.

The horse was a good form, and she enjoyed long, frequent walks with the man and being an agreeable partner. She decided that he didn't have to know every side of her; sometimes, at night, with her friends, she was the vulture, laughing raucous, ugly laughter that left her feeling free and full of life. But the man loved her, and she was happy with him in their little house surrounded by trees—or, at least, the horse form was happy.

They married quickly, and after a few months, while they were walking through the garden of their new home, he began a new conversation in a roundabout way, telling her how he loved her muscles and the way she ran, how he'd first fallen for her when he saw her sleek coat reflecting the sun. How her mane and tail flew behind her when she galloped. And he was very happy with her, and also, since they were going to be together for the rest of their lives, wouldn't it be fun—for both of them—if she introduced another form? Knowing that she could, after all, take other forms, as she'd told him once, though he'd never seen it. And, he added, he knew she had done it in a past relationship, but not for him.

What kind of form?

A swan, he said. He'd been thinking about swans lately, couldn't get them off his mind. He noticed them at the pond—which he passed daily, when he took a certain route to work—and in city gardens. They had such soft, regal, white feathers, those coy black masks, bright orange beaks. A horse was certainly a majestic creature, but a swan? He let out a soft groan of longing.

That evening, the shape-shifter looked herself over in their bedroom mirror and noticed her back swayed in a way it hadn't before, that her coat was a little rougher than she remembered. It was true a swan wouldn't age in the same way as a horse, or at least wouldn't seem to. It was just that she didn't like to transform for others. But after some thinking, she decided it would be her choice after all. A long neck and graceful body might do her good, and maybe, after all, she was doing it for herself. And so, after securing promises that her husband did still treasure her from mane to fetlocks, the shape-shifter transformed into an elegant white swan.

In the mornings, when she went foraging for worms and frogs and other delicacies, she could feel him watching her lovingly out the window. And she did feel a little more beautiful even than when she was a horse, though she couldn't run as quickly. And he was more attentive now and stroked her long white feathers as he had once stroked her mane, and he said she was more attractive than any of the other swans, had a more perfect curve to her neck, such soft, cloud-like wings, really more angel than swan.

Sometimes, her neck got twisted in the bedsheets, and her tail was uncomfortable in bed, but she liked her life as a swan, despite the quiet, nagging feeling of missing the galloping through the hillsides, and the other feeling, which was that there were still parts of herself she hid from him.

Sometimes at night while her husband was sleeping, she turned into a bat and flew out the window. She could blend perfectly into the night sky. Unseen, she banged in freedom against the eaves. Watching the stars above, catching bugs, sailing through the black summer air, she felt more agile and freer than she ever did in the daytime. Elation—a soaring off into infinity. And then at the end, she would come back because she did love and miss her husband and didn't want that soaring freedom forever, only for a little while.

Sometimes, she wished to be something grotesque, for the feel of it. Once, when her husband was out of town, she went out drinking in a dive bar as a terrible tarantula, and met with strange men who never imagined she was a woman at all, just a form, a terrible spider. That night, she bought drinks for everyone and stayed out until two in the morning, telling stories, and not once did anyone ask her to be anything other than who she was. This, later, she would recall as the happiest night of her life. At the end of the night, she embraced the men she was drinking with, using all eight hairy arms, and did not flinch when they stroked hers in return.

After she'd been a swan for a few months, her husband began to feel more absent and no longer gave the look of desire. He became agitated about the grass and beetle parts she dropped on the kitchen floor when she wasn't careful, and the sounds of her honking. One afternoon, he began to tell her again how happy she had made him, how in love with her he was, and how, wouldn't it be better—*she could feel it coming.*

They contemplated other forms. It seemed everywhere they went, she could feel him watching other birds and fish and mammals. She began to fear then that the problem, really, was her. That by sharing who she really was, and what she was capable of, she had created the situation in the first place. One night, over a plate of algae and spiders, the shape-shifter asked her husband to table the conversation of forms, and so they did. They held a party, where their friends touched her soft feathers in conversation and admired her as she circled their home in flight. At the party, too, was a little snow leopard her husband had met through friends, dappled and fierce, and she noticed his eyes resting on the leopard's haunches.

A week after the party, her husband asked the shape-shifter, apropos of nothing, whether she'd ever thought about becoming a snow leopard. She swung her long neck in his direction.

Really. A snow leopard.

He said the idea had just come to him from nowhere, and wasn't there some . . . essential sweetness and life to their love, if they could just capture it again, like they had once before . . . and snow leopards strutted with such sinuous grace, and she should show herself off more anyhow. He hadn't thought about that before with the swan suggestion—it was his fault—but another form would solve all of that.

There was something alluring about the man that had made her fall for him in the first place, that came down to his desire for her. It was a powerful feeling, being swept up in a gaze like that, most of all when she saw herself as he saw her—a gleaming horse, a regal swan, a snow leopard. She felt as though she might do anything to maintain that feeling. Sometimes it was hard to know herself at all, except through his eyes.

She began to feel the tiniest sliver of doubt and wondered, deep down, whether she had a true self. And if she did, whether the bat or the tarantula was a truer self than the horse or the swan, which were also her, but not the whole her, and if so, how she would ever tell her husband, whom she loved.

After a long fight that went into the night, she agreed to change once more, adding that after that, she wouldn't change again for him for a full year, and he shouldn't bother asking. He agreed.

In the morning, she was an emu. She relished the moment when he realized what had happened and wordlessly brought his hand to his mouth.

She liked being tall, high on spindly legs and with no iridescence or grace. She could see better out the windows of their home. She could reach all the high kitchen shelves without flying. Their friends commented she had really let herself go.

But the thing that surprised her was how happy and careless and free this form made her. She dropped berries and seeds all over, and they got buried in the textured carpet in the living room. And she found herself more affectionate toward her husband, and sought to nuzzle him in the evenings with her beak, though she could feel him growing more distant.

Eventually, the shape-shifter's husband declared he was tired of the very idea of forms, and one day, she saw him watching a woman who lived nearby, who was always herself, shaking out the rugs into her garden. And he gave that pained look of longing.

The shape-shifter decided she had no other recourse left. She would get a tattoo. The idea enthralled her, because it would mark a constant self, despite the shifting forms—something she had long desired.

The tattoo did not save the marriage, of course. Her husband left her, but the shape-shifter did love her tattoo. It was a drawing of a yellow butterfly, her favorite form, which she now adopted, and what was better than a butterfly with a tiny butterfly tattoo? She had gotten it on her stomach while she was still an emu. Her butterfly form was light and lively, and she made sure to flutter by once in the window, while her former husband and the woman were having breakfast. And she knew that he saw her, and that was all she wanted, as she embraced her new form, the emblem of shape-shifters.

The shape-shifter told the story of her tattoo over drinks with friends like this: There was once a woman who got a tattoo after falling hopelessly in love with a man who thought she was very nearly perfect—except for that which made her essentially herself. Then, she marked her stomach, to remember that essential self.

The shape-shifter found the tattoo very funny. All her friends did too, and she exposed her belly, and they poked at it, looking closer and closer to find a tiny butterfly tattoo on the tiny belly of a butterfly. It tickled, and her laughter was a happy, microscopic tinkling.

Domestication

Christopher rides over on his bike to ask if I want to visit our house before it's too late, and it might already be. The other kids are inside playing video games, watching evening cartoons, while the basketball hoops stand tall and lonely in the empty streets. But I hop on my bike, and we ride on the sidewalks, past cottontails overrunning the neighborhood, and one dashes in front of us so quickly I almost lose my balance.

The house is a tall, two-story brick home with an OPEN HOUSE sign and the smell of fresh paint inside. It is ours because we found it, claimed its dark wooden cabinets in the kitchen where we live a miniature life together, no one knocking around or blaring television or telling us to do homework, just clean lines of wood and granite inside. And outside, at the edge of a thick forest, is an oak tree with a tire swing that sways in the last rays of sunlight. The house is worth one hundred thousand dollars, and Christopher and I intend to buy it.

The house is never locked, because it wanted to be found, because no one has ever lived here before, because just six months ago it was forest too, and the forest creeps right up to its edge. Just next door is a field with tall, grassy reeds and coyotes that howl in the evenings while the neighbors walk their dogs.

The coyotes are getting bolder, creeping out sometimes at night to the edges of the neighborhood, looking for food. Christopher says Mr. Donolon has started carrying a small handgun in the evenings, tucked behind his belt, in case he sees one of them getting close. I suspect if they really do start coming closer, all the men will be out with guns, and they'll want to keep Christopher and me inside all the time too, just like the rest of them, but Christopher and I have other plans.

We will miss our families when we move into our new house, but not much, because we'll be too busy running from room to room like explorers. There is an empty bedroom, mine, with a long bay window, and a cedar closet Christopher claims as his study. Another room is for our boy, and one for our girl. Christopher and I aren't in love and don't want to be, but in this house, we are married and have two kids, each with their own bedroom. In real life, I am twelve, and Christopher is a year older and a few inches taller, and at school, I'm too shy to look in his direction.

I will not miss the constant requests from my parents to do homework, to watch my little sister, to set the table, to shower, while outside the coyotes call out and the forest lies soft and green and waiting. Sometimes I watch my mother under the fluorescent kitchen lights and wonder whether she too remembers exploring the wilderness outside her home, climbing trees with her sisters, or the time they came upon an injured hawk. Out the window sometimes at dinner, I catch rabbits hopping by and follow her eyes as they rest on them. I dream some nights I am a silent, stalking forest animal, unafraid of the night and impossible to trap.

From the upstairs guest bedroom, a window lets out to a flat section of the roof where the whole world lies before us, a landscape we know from days and days of exploring—a gully with a creek where we pull wild onions up from the ground, and sometimes by the water, under thick mud, real arrowheads.

From here, we can see all of Donolon Ranch, its gray-topped one- and two-story houses, green squares of lawn, swimming pools, freshly paved roads, and other plots of land with fresh wooden frames going up between the edge of the neighborhood and the forest.

Christopher makes me feel brave. He wrinkles his nose and says we're going to hide the fliers so no one else can buy the house, and once we buy it, we're going to make sure it's the last house anyone builds around here, and we'll stop the yellow diggers from pulling up any more stretches. And that's why despite not loving Christopher, I don't mind being pretend-married to him.

While I'm shooing away a housefly circling around us, Christopher stops talking, points his index finger toward the edge of the forest, and then I see it. A small gray-and-brown body moving forward, nose pointed, with sure, feline movements so unlike the dog it resembles. It stops for a moment when a car speeds by, disoriented briefly, looks around, and then continues on its path. Roosting crows caw from a telephone wire in the distance. The animal picks up speed a little and begins trotting, starts and stops, comes right up to the house, and slows all the way down.

Then it freezes, and we freeze with it. I feel the warm gray shingles under my legs, a soft breeze rustling my hair. I see the stretches of trees and tall grass fading from green to gray under the darkening sky. I see the coyote's figure becoming an outline that will lose its definition as the sun goes down. I know this moment will pass.

In the same way, I know these new houses, a neighborhood called Donolon Ranch after the family that bought up the whole tract in the 1930s, will look this way for only a little while. The old clay pit and brick factory will disappear, and in ten or twenty years, maybe sooner, it'll be nothing but houses and parks.

And probably Christopher and I won't grow up and get married, likely we'll meet other people and lose touch, and decades will go by, and if we see each other after that, we'll glance at each other shyly and neither of us will mention the house. Years will go by, and I imagine the edge of the forest will become a library, and the lake where white egrets roost in trees will become a public park, places to cut ribbons and take wedding pictures and go on evening walks with pets on leashes, but not places to get wild and muddy or to catch a glimpse of a bobcat at dusk. Then, Christopher and I will have to remember this place, otherwise no one will, because years from now, kids like us will walk across paved sidewalks, kids who couldn't even imagine a place like this.

And I might be a child, but I also know I'm getting too old for pretend. It is possible for me to dream of my house with Christopher and believe in it and save up for it and also not believe in it. Kids aren't stupid. I'm going to finish school, get too old and embarrassed to climb on roofs, and get married. I am so scared of that. I want to run away into the forest like the coyotes, and that's why sometimes I go out like this when I know very well my parents are at home wondering about me.

Finally, we see it, the thing the small coyote is stalking, and it's Mr. Donolon's brown dachshund. Christopher leaps to the front of the roof so quickly I'm afraid he's slipped, and then I see he's reaching for a rock in the gutter, and in a moment, his arm is up, ready to strike. We're close enough that just a little throw could probably hit the coyote, or at least scare it away. But I grab Christopher's wrist hard to tug him away from the edge, and also because I don't want him to hit the coyote.

That's all the time it takes. In a moment, the coyote lifts the dachshund by the scruff of its neck, a great whine fills the air, and in a moment, Mr. Donolon bursts out of the house in his T-shirt, shorts, and bare feet, staring left and right. But in the darkness, he sees nothing out of the ordinary, and after a moment, he returns inside.

The coyote is gone again, lost in the forest. We can only imagine it now, tearing into Mr. Donolon's poor dog, and Christopher is staring at me in disbelief, the rock still clutched in his fingers. For a second, I see his lip twitch and his eyes get hard because he missed his one shot, because of me.

I want to tell Christopher I didn't want the dog to be hurt, and I know what I did is bad, but so is hurting coyotes and tearing up their homes, and moving onto their property. I know it isn't right or fair, taking up space that isn't really ours and pretending it could be, and I know we're part of it too, and I don't see a way out.

Someday I'm going to move very far away from here, from my parents and family, and take up space somewhere new, and they might try to stop me, but I'm going to do it anyway. I think about that dog out there just beyond the forest line, maybe bleeding, maybe already gone.

Christopher puts the rock back down in the gutter, and I think he forgives me just then, because he says the coyote must've been so hungry to come so close to us. And if we were different kinds of friends, I might do something like put my hand on his, but I smile at him instead.

I'm a little sad for the dog in the end, and I'll pretend to be sadder when I tell the story to my friends tomorrow at school, leaving out the part about the house and the roof, and making them swear not to tell about the coyote. But really, I'm tired of the kids in our neighborhood who want to play video games, who want to sit inside and play with figurines, the parents who want us to do our homework and wash our hands and set the table for dinner. Christopher and I have the whole sky and forest and a house and many big and secret plans for our lives.

Christopher said once he plans to live forever in this house, taking care of the live oaks, picking up the knobby branches and sticks that litter the ground—plans I know, and he knows, because we're getting older, are just pretend, like all of this. But I don't tell him, I let him go on about his plans to tend the forest, to buy and move into this house together. We lift up our pretend children in their bedroom windows to gaze at the tall grass, as we watch it now for a little longer, as the coyotes start howling, as our parents walk up and down the sidewalks looking for us.

Proportions

Serene's family did not seem to notice when she began to shrink.

When her three children got off the school bus and came home, throwing shoes to the side and crashing around, she fit so perfectly in the hidden area between the refrigerator and the door to the outside that they looked for her only briefly. Then they poured out their crackers and cereals for snacks and went along their way to the basement.

When Charlie arrived home from work, he cocked his head to the side and said to Serene, "You look cute today," and kissed the top of her head, stooping all the way down to the floor to do it.

Serene waved her hands, asking him to keep his voice down; she didn't like the way the sound boomed and bounced through the kitchen, off the smeared trash can and the sticky fridge and all the other metal surfaces with dents—the noise, always the noise. He asked in a louder voice, "What?"

And then Serene climbed to the top of the cat bowl and shouted, "Do you notice anything different about me?" And he gave a baffled smile. "Haircut?"

Serene shook her head and finished making dinner. Somehow being small didn't stop her.

Charlie had made plans for them to visit his mother after dinner that evening. But Serene said she wasn't feeling well, and they ought to go without her. Charlie asked whether she was sure.

"Don't you notice anything different about me?" Serene repeated. Charlie seemed to be holding back a feeling, and the children seemed sad she wasn't coming. Serene said she would get them settled into the car and that she would buckle Steven, the littlest, in the back, and then she followed them out to the car, kissed them goodbye, and returned to the house with relief. She felt herself grow an inch just seeing the car disappear around the corner.

It would be a long evening, as Charlie's mother lived nearly an hour away. She expected they would drive, spend a couple hours visiting, and then return home a little before ten at night.

Serene unloaded the dishwasher, then found a leftover bowl of popcorn and dragged several pieces over to the couch. There, she mashed on the remote control and chose a serialized television drama. It was about a woman from the south of England who travels to the north, where factories have replaced the former pastoral way of life, where women and men labor over cotton looms, where the workers go on strike and children nearly starve as a result. When the drama got to the point of the strike, Serene turned it off, because she was tired of thinking about toil and feeding hungry bellies. She was tired of thinking about women who'd been overlooked in history. She was still hungry. She finished the popcorn. It was only then that she realized she was back to her normal size.

What Serene wanted most of all now was a tall glass of wine. She wished aloud for one, and then realized she must have poured herself a glass already while watching the show, because she found it waiting for her. She took it over to the couch, closed her eyes, and breathed in the smell. It was red and delicious, and the first sip felt like the wine of heaven, her glass the holy grail. She would let it turn her teeth pink, she would breathe it in, she wouldn't care about anything else for a little while.

Over the next hour, her phone was buzzing and buzzing, but Serene didn't care about that. She was reading the last chapters of a novel she had been trying to get through for an entire year. She sipped the wine and cried for the novel's heroine, who had lost her little boy. And although Serene's three children were somewhere across the city, visiting their grandmother, she somehow found it much easier to cry for the heroine's little boy, Neddy, than to miss her own. She thought of little Neddy and longed to cradle him. And then she moved over to the piano and began to play a melancholy song, making herself cry more. Then she gazed longingly at her bookshelf, picked up a short story collection, put it down, picked up another, feasting greedily on little paragraphs, ordering dish after dish, nibbling but never finishing, reveling in her freedom.

The silence was remarkable. And in that silence, too, her voice grew louder.

Because all this time alone, Serene had been growing. As she looked up from the pages, she found she had doubled her normal size. Her long legs and back no longer fit comfortably on the green velvet sofa, which was creaking under her weight.

"Oh, what is happening," she muttered to herself.

"Did you never notice?" a voice responded. It was soft, barely audible and when she looked down, she saw her own mother, coming only up to her ankle. "The glass of wine? How it appeared the moment you wanted it?"

Serene yelped in terror. The sound boomed through the house and set off a car alarm somewhere down the street. A neighborhood dog began to howl in the distance.

More quietly, she said, "I did wonder about that. But Mom! Is that really you? You died!"

"Yes, it's me, Serene."

She regarded her mother, perfectly doll-sized, with her hair in a loose bun and wire-rimmed glasses on her nose. "Did you pour the glass?"

"Yes, of course. I come in at night sometimes, straighten things out here and there. I like helping you. Though—I seem to shrink when I do it. I took the day off today."

"And I began shrinking."

"So it seems."

"Anyway—we buried you."

Serene's mother covered her ears. "A little quieter? Oh, Serene. Silly girl, I'm too busy to die. Could you imagine it? Me, running around heaven, worried about you, unable to be of any use. What kind of heaven would that be? Well, I chose this. Maybe I'm in hell." She paused a beat. "I'm joking, Serene. Shall I pour you another?"

Serene took a moment to let it all sink in. She had a crick in her neck from bending down. "Something is different about you."

"I'm tiny, Serene."

"Oh, yes." That was it. She'd known it, of course, but it hadn't clicked exactly until her mother said it. "Did it happen for you too? Is Grandma—"

Serene's mother reached into her pocket and spoke into her hand.

"Is that her? She fits in your pocket? Mom, I can't even see her."

Serene's mother paused thoughtfully. "It is odd. I suppose I never considered it. She is small, isn't she? Maybe her spine compressed with age." She added, "Mom, Serene is asking about you." She appeared to listen. "Sorry, Mom. I'll try to speak more quietly." What came from her mouth next was inaudible.

Serene's mother explained then that her own mother had not exactly died either, but instead had stuck around to help her, and of course she couldn't bear not to watch her grandchildren grow older, except they were so large and loud and incomprehensibly different that they caused her to flee to the insides of walls most evenings. And they were too large to help at any rate, so Serene's grandmother could only help her own daughter, who had to help Serene.

Serene looked closer. Her grandmother could not be seen, except with the use of a magnifying glass one of the children had left in a toy basket. And even with that, she was a speck, like an angel dancing on the head of a shoestring one of the children had left on the floor.

"Is my great-grandmother there?" Serene asked. "How far back does it go, the mothers and daughters?" Her mother nodded and then seemed to speak to her hand. They waited a long minute. "Are you still—" Serene's mother spoke quietly to her own mother, who, Serene could see through the magnifying glass, gave a magnificent shrug. "They are still asking. Each one, asking another," Serene's mother said. They waited longer. Finally, Serene's mother concluded, "We couldn't possibly know how many of us there are."

Serene had grown very large in this time. She moved from the couch to the floor, where her feet extended now almost outside the living room. She felt she was wasting precious time; her family would be gone only another couple of hours at most. Maybe it wasn't waste, exactly, though it often felt that way. There was so little time, she had to be careful to use it to the fullest. She decided to look busy. She picked up a little here and there. Not too neat—otherwise, they might expect too much of her. She closed the piano, rinsed out the wine glass and put the wine bottle away, turned off the television, and filed away the books. This minimal tidying seemed to bring her back to her proper size.

And then, too soon, they were back. She heard them before she saw them, chattering outside, the wildness waiting in the wings. And she was gripped by joy—of course there was joy in seeing them, because she loved them—but equally by dread. The quiet had already been broken, and she could notice the moonlight coming in, and the streetlights and the shadows, and soon it would be all noise and thumping and stomping, and oh, here they were. She could feel herself shrinking at a rapid pace.

There was, after all, only so much space in the house, air in the room, people who could be front and center. She retreated to the back of the kitchen.

But then they flung themselves upon her, and she noticed the little one, Steven, five, was crying, and Charlie was grabbing for an ice pack. And they shouted over each other that they'd been in an accident on the way to their grandmother's, and so they never made it there, and they'd tried to call her but she hadn't answered, and they were all right, except Steven hadn't been buckled and had been slung to the side and maybe broken his arm. She saw their sweet, plump faces, chattering over each other, and one asked for water, another for a snack.

It was just like Neddy from her book, but Steven hadn't fallen from a window, he'd been slammed against a car door, unbuckled, now crying quietly in pain. The little stoic. They would go to the hospital tonight, all together, to see about his hurt arm.

Serene rushed with them to the car and offered to drive, but Charlie said he would do it, and he tried to grab the keys from her, too roughly. Serene slammed her keys onto the hood of the car harder than she'd intended, and said, *fine*, and they were off. She spaced out in the car while the children chattered and Steven moaned quietly.

The doctor took Steven within the hour, and they measured and weighed him and took his blood pressure, and Serene noticed when they weighed him, how much he was growing. How many pounds since last time, she couldn't be sure, she was never one of those mothers who knew her children's height or weight, or even how much they'd weighed at birth, only that they were growing. The older one, his voice on the cusp of changing, hovering somewhere in between. And she liked to see the numbers go up, that they were all getting bigger, but she wished she didn't also have to get smaller.

But of course it was a zero-sum game. A mother's love wasn't infinite, like they'd told her. It could be given or hoarded for the self, but it couldn't do both. She could read the novel and play the piano, or she could put away their things. She could take her own mother's acts of service, or she could do the tasks herself and let her mother rest. It was all about finding the right combination of shrinking, growing, shrinking again, and she wasn't sure how she could ever get it right. Priorities, her mother might have called it, but to Serene, it was something more like getting the proportions right, how the needs of one measured up against another. Everything had a cost, a measurement, a gain somewhere that was a loss somewhere else. One exchange of strength for another, Serene thought, that's what love is.

After the doctor checked on Steven, while they waited to get an X-ray, Serene excused herself to the bathroom. She remembered this hospital and its hallways well. She had given birth to all of the children here. When she was first pregnant, the doctor told her not to worry too much about the nutrition, because the baby would take what he needed from her, and she was so weak those nine months she could hardly move; the sleep deprivation later was nothing at all compared to carrying a child. It was back then she should've known, must have, that all love comes with a cost. It was a bald lie that it didn't.

Along the way back, Serene stopped into a little garden just outside. She wasn't quite ready to return to the sterile hospital room. She pulled a flask from her purse, where she'd kept a little more of the wine, and let herself savor it for a quiet moment. They would be all right without her for an extra minute. Here, in the quiet alcove outside, under a black sky, surrounded by low hedges, some purple aster, the stars shining, Serene felt her heart quiet, and then she felt a stirring in her hip pocket where the flask had been and remembered her mother, who had pulled herself up to the top of Serene's pocket and was swinging a leg around to the outside.

Serene lifted her mother gently onto her palm and told her all about what had happened to Steven. Serene's mother patted Serene so gently she couldn't feel the movement, only see it, but she felt its power all the same, and it soothed her. "Steven will be all right. I'm sure of it." They were quiet for a long moment. Serene liked the little movement, the tiny pressures of her mother stretching out her legs and tickling the palm of her hand.

"Mom, why didn't I see you this way before?"

"Oh, Serene, no one ever sees her mother truly until she becomes a bit more like her mother. As you are now. Anyhow, it wouldn't be fair, to see how much you take from your mother. Children are still so little, and they need so much. They have no idea how much. And it's better not to know, isn't it? It would gut them to know what it costs to love them."

Serene shrugged. It was good to be seen now, anyway, by her mother. And what about the men? Did they shrink and grow? Serene's mother said she wasn't sure, that she'd never thought about it before, that it had been only her mother who'd rested in her hand, though it was possible a father could too, sure, why not. Maybe it's changing, this generation is so different. The men do more. Not all of them, but many.

Maybe Serene's dad preferred heaven to a life of continued service; who knew? He had certainly worked hard enough in this life, and maybe heaven would be a nice respite. Serene's mother said she did miss him, but only in the kind of way she missed him when he was watching a show in the study and she was doing the dishes in the other room. They had already spent all those years together. That was how Serene's mother explained it.

Back inside, Serene found she'd missed Steven's transfer, but a nurse walked her to the room, and she found her family just as a technician was gently positioning Steven's bruised arm on the table under the X-ray. And the brave little smile on his face when he saw Serene made her heart want to burst.

While they waited for the results, Steven rested, and the other children began to argue over a game on the iPad they had brought with them. Serene whispered for them to quiet, and felt herself shrinking again as they ignored her and bickered louder, causing a nurse passing by to poke her head into the room.

Charlie noticed the flask then in Serene's open purse, let out a deep sigh and said, "You shouldn't have brought that," and returned to his phone.

"I've shrunk again," she whispered to him. "Can you tell?"

After a pause, he said, "Did you notice? I'm diaphanous."

Serene thought Charlie might be lying about being see-through. And if he was, she suspected, he might just be doing it for attention. But now that she thought of it, she couldn't deny Charlie did seem to fade sometimes when he overextended himself. And even now, Serene could see through Charlie to a little of the color of the blue chair he was sitting on.

She remembered now how, sometimes, just before they made love, she could see completely through him, and only when they finished did he become solid again, with muscle and weight. If Charlie was becoming diaphanous and Serene hadn't noticed, that was embarrassing. And maybe it was true she wasn't observant enough about him, like when he got a new haircut, or he shaved, and Serene didn't register it.

Another family rushed by outside the room, and Serene and Charlie paused long enough to observe them and exchange a long glance. When the doctor returned, he said Steven's arm wasn't broken after all, just a nasty bruise. The doctor said they should watch him a few days though, especially since Steven said he had hit his head in the accident. Then the doctor adjusted his glasses and asked in a quiet voice, "Was he buckled?"

And Charlie looked at Serene's feet, and Serene stared at her own and tried and tried to remember whether she had done it when she had followed them to the car and said she would, or whether someone else might've done it for her. But as she tried to conjure the moment, and Steven's little face, all she could remember was the relief at the quiet, and the staying home, and she couldn't remember what her fingers had or hadn't done with the buckle, only the way she'd felt afterward. She tugged at her wedding ring and said, "Should have been," and neither she nor Charlie would look at the other. When Serene reached into her pocket again, her mother was gone. Oh, where had she gone, just when Serene needed her most?

The doctor said he thought Steven would probably be all right but that they ought to watch for headaches and changes in vision and other signs. They were quiet on the drive home. Charlie said he'd put the kids to bed, and Serene stared at the house and wondered what to make of it. It looked, once more, like a tornado had hit it. She was small again, too small and tired to make a dent in the mess. They would need to get the car repaired too after the accident, to get it checked out at the very least, so now there was an inspection, and the list went on and on.

And then Steven gave a little wave to his mother as he passed by on the way to his bedroom. Steven, stocky and solid and growing. All those meals packed into him.

Serene had trouble, sometimes, telling her children she loved them. She tried to make herself enjoy moments with them, tried to treasure them, only she felt so small, and it was difficult to articulate any particular moment to treasure. She wasn't sure why it was so difficult to put into words. Their voices were so loud and so urgent that it was so often difficult to form a thought at all. Often, it was easier to do something for them.

She poured another glass of wine and sipped, and it was only then, with the pleasant warmth in her body, and all of them gone into other rooms, that she could feel herself start to come alive and grow again. It was easier to love from a distance, from a book, on the page, after some wine.

Maybe, Serene thought, she really was distant and forgetful, but she did pick up their little things and drive them places and check what boxes she could. And if her heart wasn't always in it, well she'd at least accomplished some of the tasks to help them along before they inevitably eased away from her.

Serene knew the children would be gone someday, and sometimes she wondered whether she'd be a better mother then. She thought of a mother at the children's school who had never missed a school recital or a parent-teacher conference, and wondered why she couldn't be that kind of mother. Serene was sorry she wasn't that mother, and sometimes, she suspected she was on the verge of becoming like another, better, mother. But most of the time, she was mustering through. Serene, for a brief moment, wondered whether her own mother had ever felt that way, and why the thought had never before occurred to her.

Serene moved to empty the dishwasher and was surprised to see it mostly empty. She felt a surge of affection toward Charlie. Then, she vaguely remembered having done it herself earlier in the evening. It couldn't have been her mother, because her mother hadn't been there at that moment. Serene was the one who had unloaded the dishwasher. She had herself to thank. But, if that was true, if Serene really was the one responsible, then Serene had also been the one who had forgotten to buckle Steven. She couldn't blame that on anyone but herself.

The older two children rushed into the kitchen just as the thought was sinking in. The boy said he had been promised the first chance at a shower, the girl said he would use all the hot water if he got there first, and couldn't they put him on a timer? She said Serene had promised to put them to bed too, and Serene had, but now, surveying the mess of the house, she wanted to find a way out of it.

As Serene tried to hold a clear thought about what to do next, she began to shrink at a terrible rate. She could see the children, looming, waiting for answers about the showers and bedtimes. She could hear Steven in the other room begging Charlie for another story, and she regretted that it wasn't her he asked for. In that moment, what Serene wished for more than anything in the world was to tuck her three children tenderly into bed. But she was shrinking too quickly, slipping along the counter. She grabbed onto a cork for dear life. Serene wished desperately for someone, anyone, to hold her and slow her descent, but there was no hand or seat belt to be found, only the skidding of the cork across the countertop, closer and closer to the edge.

Before All That

In the end, she sells me for a hundred dollars. She doesn't stop to think it over, doesn't caress my head a last time with her thumb. She plinks me onto the glass countertop and takes the bill. "Women in this market usually go for larger karats," says the woman at the pawnshop with the nails filed down to pink nubs.

Before that, the woman's husband lost Gold Band in a parking lot after another fight. He'd wanted to see how Gold Band felt in his jacket pocket. They were both waiting to see if they would need a replacement after Gold Band.

The last time I saw Gold Band was the time he went rummaging through their things before packing a suitcase to go somewhere without us. I was living in her top dresser drawer then. I didn't see much of Gold Band during that time, but I thought of him constantly. In that time, she said she hated how I felt against her skin. She stopped eating regular meals, lost weight, and her fingers shrank. When she did wear me, she spun me around endlessly with her thumb, making me dizzy.

Years before that, she almost lost me. She went out without the man, got drunk, and waved her hands around, telling stories. I slipped off and clinked onto a sticky bar floor next to crumbs of fried batter. We spent a lot of time in that bar, never any of it with Gold Band. I had always assumed if one of us would be lost, it would be me.

Gold Band was simple and hammered smooth and reflected light in every direction. I first met Gold Band on a satin pillow in a small church. It wasn't love at first sight; it took us years to get used to each other. We were never on the two hands that held each other—but Gold Band reflected the light perfectly and had an etching down his middle that made the most delicious scratching sound against the man's thumbnail. Once, when they were reaching across the table to hold hands, we clinked together. It was a ding like the sounds of heaven. I could tell Gold Band was falling for me too, even if he didn't say it.

Before that, the man put me in a small black box in his jacket pocket, which he pulled out at a restaurant by the ocean. The waves rose and fell endlessly next to our table, and I longed to touch the water but didn't because just then, he got down on one knee. She looked at me with wild delight—*me*—and said yes. Before that, he checked and rattled the bulge in his jacket pocket a dozen times.

Before that, his mother gave me to him. I'd thought she would keep me, because before that, she too had said *I do*. Before Gold Band, there was Yellow Gold, with milgrain beading around his edges. Yellow Gold had been to war and back and had a few nicks from the experience, but I told him—and I meant it—that shopkeepers knew nothing of true value.

Before that, a jeweler mounted me onto a slender gold setting, with small claws above a gold circle that wrapped around and then became part of me. There's something divine in being joined together like that. I sat that way for a long time in a glass case under a hot fluorescent bulb waiting for someone to notice the way I let the light shine through me.

Before that, the jeweler explained to her apprentice that the light shining through me meant love, that gold had meant power and immortality in ancient cultures, and that diamonds were chosen because we seem to resist any tarnish or chips, although I didn't choose to be who I am, and if truly pressed, I'd say *if* love is forever, where is Yellow Gold, and if second love is possible, why not Gold Band, and what these impossibly tender humans could never understand is that their strength is in their soft forgetfulness. Being made of a hard and unforgiving substance means carrying too many lives of memories on our surfaces.

Before that, a boy with feet caked in clay found me in a wooden sieve. That was after many years of lying under the earth, deep within a fiery mantle. I still think of his puffy cheeks, his tiny fingers, how he gazed at me and gulped.

Regression

The other seventh-grade girls are worried Olivia has really lost it this time. First, there was Ginny's sleepover party—Ginny, who wet herself last year in the sixth grade, which no one has forgotten. Olivia went to her party, alone, with a two-liter bottle of ginger ale, Ginny's favorite. Ginny's dad says the girls stayed up past midnight watching a Disney movie, and rumor has it Olivia returned home with Mickey Mouse-shaped cookies from Ginny's house. They say she pulled one out at lunch, and the other girls scooted their chairs to the next table over because the cookie might have had pee on it. Olivia, who once could've sat at any lunch table at all. One of the girls spotted Olivia's mascara in a trash can in the girls' locker room. Her lip gloss hasn't surfaced in days. Now, she has the nerve to show up to Algebra barefaced. Mr. Bond is explaining linear regression. Olivia asks Mr. Bond to explain it one more time. He says it's a way of understanding values. The idea is that the value of a point or line depends on the others around it. Put another way, you gauge what the other points are doing and try to fit your line in. The other girls exchange looks when Olivia speaks. One of them has taken to twirling her hair in the way Olivia does, for laughs. Mr. Bond watches Olivia's face to see if she got it, but he isn't sure. Olivia is getting worse at keeping up with the girls' banter. She is tired of YouTube and TikTok and thinks some of the memes are a little mean. She's reading a graphic novel Ginny lent her about dragons and a girl with magical powers. There is a danger she could get lost in it or, worse, start to believe she has powers. Olivia's oldest friends think an intervention is in order. They'll invite Olivia over for a makeover and a rom-com and warn her of the dangers of talking to Ginny. Ginny has been turning back into a baby since the start of the school year, and now the girls feel it's contagious. It might even be too late. If Olivia isn't careful, she might never grow up.

Clementine

Clementine didn't know any children's songs. That was the first thing that struck me as odd about her, and it stuck with me even after she was gone and buried. I didn't see how it was possible that she couldn't recall hearing a single one.

We were all eighteen, about to graduate high school, but she seemed older, with a brave pixie haircut, a small face, the cheeks of an angel, and one small nose piercing, although her parents would have let her have as many as she wanted. She had a debit card with her name on it—her real name, Crystal Dorn—and a job at the diner after school.

She haunted me the summer after high school, in the long, sticky evenings when the crickets came out and the ghosts started moving through town. I sat alone at the diner where Clementine used to work. It was a cavernous place set inside a hundred-year-old brick building. In the daytime, you could see out the windows across the river a bald slag of rock that stuck out over the green hills and the valley that was filling up with the land taken off the top.

The diner was never very full. Our town was losing people, bleeding them into the bigger cities around us—Roanoke, Lexington, Johnson City—anywhere somebody could get a job. Maybe no one wanted to be here in the first place.

What Clementine was doing with me, a clean-cut JROTC guy, was beyond me. I wasn't the type of guy girls in our high school usually went for. Like the others in the Marine Corps JROTC, once a week I wore a uniform to school—a long jacket with gold buttons, slacks creased in the front, and shiny black shoes. The uniform made me feel like a hero from an old war movie. But it didn't make me popular. I couldn't help that I called the teachers sir and ma'am. The other guys seemed to keep their distance on uniform days, and more than once I'd heard a conversation stop when I got within earshot.

But Clementine could hold a whole room of us in thrall and sometimes talked so fast we couldn't understand her. Her stories about the miners and truckers who tried to pick her up at the diner had us howling in the mornings at school.

I worked hard at entertaining Clementine, too. I said anything that occurred to me just to fill space. I saved up stories, and once, when there was nothing else to say, I started singing "London Bridge Is Falling Down," and she told me she'd never heard the song. After that, I couldn't stop teasing her, calling her my fair lady, Oh Susannah, Oh My Darling, Clementine, anything I could think of. Clementine was the name that stuck. Her real name, Crystal, was too plain, so I never called her that.

I'd stand around talking to her after school sometimes, and once, right after I'd finished teasing her, she said her truck was broken and asked if I could give her a ride sometime. After that, nearly every afternoon, I dropped Clementine off at work and picked her up after her shift in the evening to drive her home.

When I picked Clementine up after her shifts, I met her in the diner parking lot so I didn't end up smelling like cigarettes and french fries the way she did. One night in early spring, after I'd been driving her for a few weeks, her shift manager—a man with a flannel jacket and a double chin—approached us.

"Your boyfriend?" he asked Clementine. An orange light hung over an awning next to a half-open dumpster with cardboard boxes sticking out. He crossed his arms, worked his jaw, and regarded me like a bull ready to gore me.

I waited to see what her answer would be.

"He's my friend. Come on, Will." And I followed.

Clementine made me deliriously happy. Just a look, a brush of her arm, could send my mind spinning, longing to touch her, dreaming about taking her to the prom. She wasn't my girlfriend, though, and the truth was that I hadn't asked because I wasn't sure what she'd say.

We drove away from the parking lot toward the lower part of town. Before midnight, a thick fog would cover the roads. We drove to a little green area next to the river, a quiet pull-off where we had started parking after her shift. We could just make out the black water in front of us. A few weeks earlier, there had been a spill, and the coal slurry made the river black and thick.

"We used to swim there as kids," I said, looking out at the flat water.

Our mayor had declared it clean, but the sludge still coated the riverbed for miles around. The newspaper said the damage was already done. Apparently, trying to dredge a river might only stir up worse toxins, so there was nothing to do but wait it out.

Clementine stared out the window at something I couldn't see.

"Feels like someone watching us," she said.

"Just a ghost," I teased. Then she reached into her pocket and pulled out a joint.

I told her I didn't know how to smoke, expecting her to laugh, but for all the teasing I did, she rarely teased me back. She lit it, inhaled, and passed it to me. "Don't get your spit on it," she said. Then I took a puff and inhaled its musty scent.

After we finished smoking, she moved over to the driver's side and wrapped her legs around me, and we kissed until my curfew. I envied her ability to come and go as she liked, while I had to be home at ten sharp on weeknights, midnight on weekends, and not a minute late.

The more time I spent with Clementine, the more friends I accumulated. She had perched on my car one afternoon after school, and like magic, her friends—soccer and football players and a few girls from the drill team—had started spending time with us too.

From the roof of my Taurus after school, you could see the bare mountaintops, shaved clean like cadets. In our parents' generation, the miners had gone deep into the caverns, but now it was cheaper to blow the tops off the hills altogether.

One afternoon, everyone was talking about a girl named Amanda. I remembered her as a smart girl with long black hair and skinny eyebrows. She'd graduated the year before us, nearly at the top of her class. She was working as a hotel receptionist and saving for college.

A blast went off somewhere in the hills, and I felt the car rumble underneath us. I rubbed my finger on the hood. It was always covered in dust.

"What?" I said to Clementine after the noise subsided.

"She overdosed, Will. Her mom found her this morning."

A few days later, Clementine asked to stop by her house on the way to work because she'd forgotten to bring a change of clothes to school. I came inside to wait for her. Her family lived in a little house, barely bigger than a trailer, set on one of the hills that rolled up and down through town.

Her mom was a nurse and worked weeknights at the hospital. Clementine's dad didn't drive because he'd injured his legs years ago, when Clementine was a baby; a piece of metal came off a hook in one of the mines, pinning him for hours. I learned that only much later, from a friend of hers, because she never spoke about it. Her friend said that once, when she was a toddler, Clementine had wandered all the way down the street before her parents realized she was gone.

The house was set right up against a busy road and shook when cars rumbled by. The inside smelled of mold and had a thousand knickknacks—tiki statues, Japanese masks—from places I was sure her parents had never been and never would go. I could see then why Clementine was so at home in that cavern of a diner.

Her dad had a drawn face, like he could've been her grandpa. I couldn't see his legs because of the blanket he had over his lower half while he watched a baseball game and nursed a Budweiser. But it was his eyes I remember, hazel and lifeless. They flitted to me, and he said hello and then went right back to the game, like it was the most important thing in the world, although it was only spring training.

Beside him on the coffee table was an unopened newspaper. On the front page was a story about the local energy company laying off workers.

Clementine's dad got up to use the bathroom, leaning on a cane. When he was out of sight, Clementine reached for a prescription bottle sitting on an end table, took a handful of pills, and stashed them in her purse.

When she saw me watching, she twisted a lock of hair around a finger. "Standing all evening hurts my back," she mumbled. "Don't look at me like that."

I would have said more, but I had a plan that evening, and I couldn't have her mad at me. I was going to ask her to prom.

~

At the end of Clementine's shift that night, I walked into the diner, even though I hated the way it smelled. She glanced around and said we could sit for a minute.

I ordered a milkshake, and she got black coffee. After the drinks came, I got so nervous I could hardly drink. She'd started spending time with some of the burnouts at school, guys who cut classes in the middle of the day to sit under the bleachers and smoke. Maybe one of them had already asked her.

She smiled a little now, knowing something was coming. She narrowed her eyes and set her lips in a line.

"Will you go to prom with me?" I blurted out.

"Oh, Will. You're so formal. You didn't have to go to all this trouble. I was gonna say yes. You practically got down on one knee."

"You were gonna say?"

"Yes, Will." She swept her bangs out of her eyes.

I could hardly breathe.

"Is your family going to do the whole picture thing? Make you pose? Expect you home by midnight?"

"Yeah," I muttered. "So dumb."

"Yeah." She rolled her eyes, but they were red and watery, and she looked like she might cry.

~

By spring, the crowd in the parking lot after school was getting thinner. Some of Clementine's friends had moved away. Others dropped out of school. In the beginning of the year, I had parked in the back of the lot, but now sometimes I got a spot right up front. Mostly, I couldn't remember who used to park there.

I must have gone to a dozen parties since I'd started spending time with Clementine. I had started sitting with her friends at lunch. I still saw my old JROTC friends, but mostly on drill days, and almost never at lunch anymore. My parents even remarked on how often the phone rang for me now at home.

By this time, everyone called her Clementine. Sometimes she argued or frowned at it, but it was a pointless gesture, and eventually she gave up.

When I picked her up on prom night, Clementine didn't want me to come inside her house. She stood on the edge of the street and waved when I pulled up.

She looked petite and frail, in a yellow lace dress that stopped at her calves. She seemed to have lost weight. Her pixie cut was growing out, so she'd pinned the sides of her hair with bobby pins. She looked like a stunning, yellow 1920s flapper with a pale face and ruby lips.

Clementine was quiet as she entered my house for the first time. Then I started to see it through her eyes: the clean white paint, a tall living room, the long counters in the kitchen.

My grandfathers had been miners, but Dad had gotten lucky and found a job at the electric plant outside of town. Mom worked there too, as a receptionist. I planned to do even better.

We made small talk for a while. I'd wanted to show my parents I was with the coolest and most beautiful girl at school, but suddenly she seemed unable even to answer the most basic questions. When Dad asked her about her job and teachers, Clementine clammed up and could barely get a word out.

Mom offered to put down Clementine's purse for the pictures, but she snatched it back. Then she put it on the couch but kept her eyes on it the whole time.

Clementine and I stood in front of the fireplace, just the way I always had for school pictures growing up. I felt sharp and confident in my rented tux.

Mom held the camera, trying to get a clear picture. But every time, it came out a blur. Finally, Dad took the camera, and after several tries, there was a slightly less blurry one, and he said, "It's all right. Make sure your friends get pictures too."

Clementine excused herself to the bathroom. The light turned golden as the day drained away. When Clementine came out, she looked bright and happy again and started talking to Mom. While they spoke, Dad stuck fifty dollars in my shirt pocket for dinner and told me just to give him the change. I couldn't believe it.

We were still early for dinner, but Clementine was ready to go, so we got in my car. She smelled of perfume and the cigarette she was smoking with the window rolled down, and I was happy to be beside her.

"Let's go to the old shack," she said. She smiled, like she was letting me in on a secret.

We still had half an hour before dinner. We passed a gas station, a warehouse, and an empty lot near the woods. The fog was beginning to settle in for the evening.

"We could, I guess." I was saying okay to whatever Clementine wanted now, because I was going to ask her that night to be my girlfriend.

As the sun dipped below the horizon, I felt the rush and excitement of a cool spring breeze. Crickets chirped, and fireflies started to appear. There was a feeling of freedom around the corner—graduation. It was intoxicating.

I followed Clementine up a hill into the woods and to a small wooden shack on the side of a dirt road. It used to be a full bar before it was shuttered up sometime when our grandparents were kids. I had only ever seen it from the road. It was the kind of thing you drove by at night to scare yourself, but no one I knew had gone in person. In front of the shack, we crossed over a railroad that still carried coal across state lines.

The shack was supposed to hold the ghost of a man who developed lung disease in the mines and couldn't support his family any longer, so he drank himself to death in the bar. As the story went, a young girl from our parents' generation had gone into the shack once and never returned. They said the old man was so lonely he took her and kept her with him. It was just a stupid thing everyone said, but it still gave me chills. I'd never have gone into the place if Clementine hadn't insisted.

While I was trying to jimmy a lock on the door, Clementine walked around to the side of the shack, where the wood had rotted away and left an opening just big enough for us to fit inside. I was shaking by now.

"Come on, Will," she said.

"You've been here before?"

She smiled too easily.

She wouldn't have judged me harshly for turning around, but I would have judged myself. What kind of future Marine was too scared to go into a little wooden shack? So, in I went.

Inside was pitch black, but I had a cell phone to use as a flashlight. There was a little bar and some tables built into the ground, but no chairs. Clementine leaned up against the bar, and turning on her full accent, said, "Let me get you a drink, darlin'." Then she reached into her bag and pulled out one lukewarm can of Budweiser—all she could fit into her purse. I laughed in delight. We popped it open and shared long swigs.

At every sound from outside, I jumped, terrified something would come for us. I was thinking about the old ghost story. Then I leaned over Clementine like I was an old cowboy at a saloon, and even through my fear, I looked at her breasts in that pale yellow dress and hoped this would be the night she'd agree to go further with me.

I knew I wasn't really her type. If I hadn't had the car, she might never have given me the time of day in the first place. But given that it was just me and the ghosts, I put my arm around her and offered an imaginary bartender a dollar for another beer.

"Bartender, what's your name?" she said, getting in on the act.

"His name is Tom," I said. And I began singing, "Have You Seen the Ghost of Tom?" But Clementine rolled her eyes, and I stopped before I could even get to the part about his skin being all gone. I could see every flicker of expression on her face through the light on my phone, shining from the bar counter.

"Just a dollar for Tom? And no tip?" she asked in pretend outrage.

I shook my head. "No. The service was shit."

She punched my arm hard. "Asshole. You always tip the waitstaff."

Only once the whole time we were in the shack did Clementine look afraid. It was just as we were draining the last of our beer, and the wind picked up and whistled sharply through the slats of wood, and she drew toward me. She clutched my jacket and looked at me with frightened eyes, but I forgot all about her and started to scramble outside, until she said, "Will! Will!"

Then I looked back at her with a flush of shame so deep I thought I would die. She saw and laughed, and said, "Those old stories are hilarious, aren't they?"

We squeezed back through the rotten spot in the wall. She adjusted a bobby pin in her hair and smoothed her dress. "Do you worry about what happens next? After graduation?"

"No. I'm going to college. And the Marines," I said. I had plans to start at the state college and ROTC with a full scholarship. But I saw from her face that wasn't what she'd meant, and then I wasn't sure what she'd meant at all.

"Marine?" She wrinkled her nose. "You were afraid of a little old shack."

We kissed, but it wasn't the same. I was too ashamed. She closed her lips and drew away. The wind whistled through the shack, and we listened to the rush of trucks going by. It was almost time for our dinner reservation. I still wanted to ask her to be my girlfriend, but it seemed the moment for that had passed.

"Did you hear that?" Clementine said.

"It's the wind again."

"I swear to God it was someone whispering," she said. "Let's go."

"Okay, Clementine."

"My name is Crystal," she said. "It's Crystal, Will. Goddammit."

Clementine was tired all through dinner. She slumped on one arm and could barely keep herself awake. She said she wasn't hungry, refused to order a full meal, and nibbled on a side of vegetables.

"What's wrong?" I asked finally.

She pushed a carrot around her plate with a fork. "My dad's old company is going under. They can't pay pensions anymore."

I let out a breath. It wasn't about us. "You'll be fine," I said, because I didn't know what else to say. "We'll all graduate soon and get out." Clementine shrugged.

As we waited for the check, a brown moth fell onto our table from a nearby open window. It was missing a wing, so it circled around aimlessly on the table, neither flying nor stopping, unable to move out of its small circle. I couldn't stand to look at it, so finally I pushed it onto the floor with a napkin and put it out of its misery with my shoe.

"Damn it, Will."

My eyes widened. "What? That was a mercy killing," I said. I hadn't done anything wrong, but she looked at me like I was a brute. It was just a moth. It left a brown smudge on the floor next to my shoe. Clementine stared down at it for several seconds like she was hypnotized.

⁂

Two of Clementine's friends won prom king and queen and wore plastic tiaras. We danced on a wooden floor as flashing strobe lights and music pulsed around us.

Clementine still seemed tired, but rallied for the dancing, and she was divine. For a few brief songs, she and I spun together in the middle of the floor, and I felt the closest I'd ever felt to heaven. Everyone around us clapped and cheered. Someone yelled, "Go, Marine!" and some of the JROTC guys I used to spend time with yelled their approval.

In the middle of it, I started to feel nostalgic, like I was already far away and looking back from some distance. I wanted to burn the scene into my memory—the flashing lights, Clementine shaking her hips and tossing her head—and save it for later, maybe after I had a wife and family of my own in a big city somewhere. But even then it was a blur.

I forgot that Clementine didn't love me or want me, or really, I didn't care in the moment. She and the dancing and my desire were intoxicating. I never wanted to go back ever again to the way I'd been before meeting her. It was only later that evening I realized her pupils were dilated beyond belief. And when I caught a glimpse of an orange medicine bottle in her open purse on the way home, I looked away.

I kept driving Clementine to and from her job, but I could feel her slipping away. We stopped kissing after her shifts ended. She made excuses not to talk on the phone. Sometimes at school when she saw me in the hallways, she'd laugh too hard at something a friend was saying and pretend she hadn't seen me.

I didn't mention my college plans. I could see she didn't want to talk about it.

"I'll visit you next year," I said one night. "I could drive up on weekends. I won't even have a curfew." I still hadn't asked her to be my girlfriend.

"Will," she said, in that way that made her seem so old. "No."

My heart sank. "Is this about the car, then? You'll ditch me when you get your own? Are you using me?"

She paused and tilted her head. "I could ask you the same thing," she said, "But since you asked, I am saving up for a car. A nicer one than yours."

"That's ridiculous. You should save your money."

"You think I'm an idiot? I know how money works. I still want a new car."

She wasn't dumb. I knew that. I could see her whole family struggling, barely able to take care of themselves. And I didn't have an answer for her. Nor could I bring myself to stop driving her, even when I still wanted her and knew in my gut she didn't feel the same.

Clementine found new friends to spend time with after school. She skipped work sometimes without telling me, so I waited for her, but she didn't show or answer her phone. She was fighting terribly with her mother and once or twice asked me to drop her off at a friend's house instead of her own at the end of the night.

Then one night while I was waiting for her in the diner parking lot, her shift manager knocked on my car window. When I rolled it down, he leaned his meaty head forward and said, "Are you taking care of her, or are you part of her problem?" I shook my head, not knowing what he meant. "Are you her dealer?" he spat out.

"Dealer? I'm helping her," I said.

He worked his jaw. "Are you?"

When she came out a minute later, she had a full tote bag slung over one arm. With the other, she handed him an apron, and he told her not to come back until she got clean. Then he gave me a final parting glare.

I knew our time was over after she lost the job. She didn't need me to drive, and in a sense, I didn't need her anymore either. I was popular at school on my own merits. As it turned out, no one else needed Clementine either. I heard that her waitress spot was filled within the hour.

A part of me wanted her to see me at graduation, surrounded by friends. When they called my name, I got some of the loudest and longest claps of anyone. But she wasn't there. Her name wasn't even on the list.

She'd died of an overdose with only weeks to go before graduation. When I heard the news from a friend, I thought about her mom and her dad, sitting with his spaced-out eyes, and that bottle of pills, and wondered how on earth I hadn't worried more about her.

Her manager's question would haunt me all summer, and, I fear, might for the rest of my life. But on that last night I drove her home from the diner, the first thought in my mind was that there must be a way to save her job, and then the second, which quickly followed, was that in fact I was as naïve as an eighteen-year-old ever could be, for thinking everything would be fine. It wasn't just the drugs. She'd been disappearing slowly from my life since the moment I'd met her.

I'd been working on a calculus set for homework while waiting for her to get off work. She picked up a page of my homework from the passenger-side floorboard and said, "So you think you're an engineer or something?" She had a cruel look, and I could see the end was near for us. But then she reached for a cigarette from her bag and said, "I'm only joking."

The whole city was disappearing. Everywhere I looked was another shuttered storefront. Whole blocks were emptying out. I was trying to decide when it all had happened, like trying to reconstruct a crime scene, and whether any of it could've been stopped if I, or anyone, had been paying attention.

The night sky was warm and filled with the sound of crickets. The stars were out. A brown moth fluttered into the car and landed on my arm, tickling me. I shooed it out and closed the window

"Will you get another job?" I asked.

"I'm not going to be able to save for the car," she said. And then after a minute, "There isn't anything up ahead, is there, Will?" She rubbed her face with her palms, a nervous gesture, like she was trying to rub off every speck of dust that might ever have found its way into her eyes and cheeks. I focused on the pitch-black road, with only the occasional shimmer of a headlight on a distant hill above us.

We drove on in silence until she said, "Sing me one of those songs."

So I leaned in at a stoplight and kissed her cheek and sang the lyrics to one of my favorites, the way my mother sang to me.

Near a cavern across a canyon,
Excavating for a mine,
Lived a miner, forty-niner,
And his daughter Clementine.

It was a silly song. I wanted her to laugh. But when I got to the chorus, she started to cry.

Skin Like Snake

Colette waits tables and writes dramatic poetry in a notebook she keeps hidden. She tries—but fails—to publish a single poem. Once, she writes, "I wish to shed my skin like a snake and become someone else." When the other waitresses find the notebook behind a cutting board, she pretends not to know whose it is. They take turns reading passages in cruel voices. When the notebook finds Colette, she laughs derisively. "Someone's shit writing," she says, emerging from her skin—cold and wet and new.

Nine Hundred Miles to Tampa

When the phone lights up again, Kevin takes in a breath and answers. "My name is Kevin Dwyer. How may I service you?" Hannah, on her own call at the next desk over, spits into the phone. The official script, pasted next to Kevin's desk, says, *How may I be of service?* Kevin grins back at Hannah.

The woman on the other end of the line, who doesn't seem to notice the screwup, wants a sporty two-door for a week. Kevin faces monitors all around him. They all do, all two dozen or so representatives, boxed into four-desk pods, each facing the others, so if they look up from their screens, they can see their faces, headsets, the backs of monitors. Hannah calls it their corner suite. Anyone walking by Kevin's desk can see he's got two screens up, and one of them is his iPad, where he's watching some guy streaming himself playing video games on Twitch. Hannah raises an eyebrow across from him, and Kevin, sensing someone passing by behind him, puts the iPad down and returns to his reservation screen. When they pass, he bobs his head and makes the rock-and-roll hand sign to Hannah.

Maybe Kevin could've been a YouTube star, with a mic in the corner of the screen and the game projected behind him. He watches guys getting rich from it. He can make his voice like theirs. He's always liked building things. Minecraft when he was younger. Planet Coaster, too. He likes checking inventories of tools, chats popping up around him. That's how Hannah described this job to him—headphones, inventories, and chats—but it's nothing like that really. He's been duped.

When Kevin asks which location, the woman on the phone says Fort Lauderdale, airport location.

"Fort Lauderdale. Yeah." He chews on a wad of gum. "Something sporty. I'll check the inventory. Yeah, west coast of Florida, a real place to be seen. Cultural capital of America, and all."

Kevin used to want to visit Florida, Disney World if he could ever afford it, but not now. He'd need a car seat anyway. He's thinking about the kind of person who can afford a week in Florida with a sporty two-seater, no car seat, just road and beaches. He thinks about his old Toyota, windows peeling at the edges, with milk spill stains on the seats and an empty baby bottle on the floor.

"It's on the east coast of Florida, actually."

"Ah, the other side of America's great wang." Amber's somewhere in Tampa now, where she has family. He thinks about her, driving on her own, no car seat ever. Just an easy, big, clean car, clean floorboards, it really burns him up. How she didn't even want custody, even ask for it. Didn't respond to his calls or emails.

"Um."

Hannah nods toward him. She's making some gesture with her headset. Kevin glances behind him, but there's no one there. The iPad is already down.

"I guess you're not on site," the voice says. "Or you're confused about which coast we're on?"

Kevin laughs. "I'm often confused, but nah." Kevin's pants feel uncomfortable all of a sudden. He sticks a hand in his pocket and pulls out a pacifier. "Damn," he says. That's where it went. He was looking all morning.

"Sorry."

"Uh, nah, we're in a call center based in Sterling. It's in Virginia."

"If I reserve a specific model, can you be *sure* it'll be there on the lot?"

Kevin remembers how Amber told him where she was going, almost as an afterthought. And then, *boom*, gone the next day. She would've had to rent a car too, since she was always borrowing his. The planning. That was what got him. She'd had to do all that without telling him. Maybe she did it online. Or maybe she called a reservation center. Or, *God*, maybe she called Quick Car. He was working here then. What if he'd answered her call? What would he have said? What if he gave her the idea in the first place?

"There'll be a car there, yes ma'am, for sure."

"How about a Porsche Boxster? We'd like to drive it to Tampa. Can I do it one way?"

"Tampa. Tampa, really? Oh, yeah, a Porsche," Kevin says. "Gotta impress some dumb prick, right?"

"Excuse me?"

There's a click.

Another woman's voice breaks in. "Ma'am, this is Regina Clark, manager at Quick Car Rental reservations. I'm going to help you find the vehicle of your choice and provide a discount for your trouble. Kevin, you may drop the call." He taps the button and he's off the call.

Hannah is staring at him. She mouths, *What happened?*

He's half-laughing, he can't help himself. It's so shitty. Everything is funny to him right now, because what can he do?

"I tried to tell you," Hannah says. "Regina's listening in today. What'd you think this meant?" She gestures to her earpiece.

"Oh it's too late. Dammit," Kevin says, the whole thing sinking in now. "Dammit. I thought you were just excited about some dumb thing you saw online or something." Kevin likes Hannah. Mostly as a friend, he thinks, though that doesn't stop him from fantasizing a little sometimes. He wouldn't have talked to her just a year ago in high school. She and Amber were in different circles. While he and Amber were smoking blunts after classes, Hannah was studying for AP physics. Now, Hannah's taking a year to save for college, Amber's in Tampa, and Kevin . . . is still figuring out what Kevin's up to.

Hannah laughs. "Goodbye, Kevin. It's been good working with you." He doesn't crack a smile.

"Hannah Hernandez. I hardly knew ye." He picks up his bag, iPad, framed picture of Mason. He stuffs it all in his bag. Just in case.

He's barely zipped his bag when Regina approaches and asks him to come with her. He follows her across the crowded den of desks into her office. An office with a door—that would be nice. If he couldn't work for himself, which would be the best option, Kevin would like his own office someday. He'd close the door, tell everyone he was on calls, and take a nap in the afternoon. He is tired. So, so, so tired

"Kevin," she says as he sits across her desk from her. Regina is not all bad. In fact, Kevin thinks, as he stares at her thick fingers and unpolished nails, she's pretty nice. He would've fired himself long ago, but there's the matter of the baby, and that seems to have kept him on. "Today's call."

"Oh. That."

"We can't have that—ever again."

"Yeah, that's fair."

"I know you've been through a lot lately." She motions to her mouth and points at him. Kevin knows gum isn't allowed on calls. He spits the gum out into his hand and then looks around for a place to toss it. She grabs a tissue and holds her hand open. Regina has three kids in elementary school. He bets she does that with them. What is it about having kids that turns you into a person who doesn't care about having someone's spit in your hand? Kevin's almost nineteen, but he feels like a kid. He drops his gum into the tissue in her hand, and she throws it away under the desk.

"Kevin, do you want this job?" He hesitates. "All right. Go home. I'll say you went home sick. Think about it, and then let's talk."

"Thank you, ma'am."

He's never called her ma'am before, and he thinks she's about to change her mind when she shrugs. "If you don't want to be here, I can't help you." Then her face softens. "How is Mason?"

"Good. He's with my parents now."

"You know, Kevin. You had a pretty good record before all this. You need another way to deal with things. Sometimes you just have to sit down and have a cry and let it all out."

Kevin crosses his arms and raises an eyebrow. "I don't cry. Never have."

Kevin's parents' house is only a mile away from the call center. When Kevin walks in the front door, Mason is whimpering in a bassinet in the living room.

Early on, Kevin couldn't believe the sound his newborn made—a shaking, quivering sound that opened something up inside him. It was so high-pitched. Now, four months into it, Kevin knows every cry. When he's hungry, it's one thing. When he's in pain, like the time Kevin accidentally dropped his iPhone on Mason's head, it's high-pitched. There's a whole lexicon of baby cries. He hears them night and day, different sounds, one after the other. Sometimes at night when the baby's not crying, he hallucinates cries and peeks over the edge of the bed into the bassinet to be sure.

Because it's Saturday, Kevin's dad is in the kitchen making a sandwich. Kevin's dad is an outdoorsman but spends every day in an office crunching numbers.

"Thought you said you'd be home tonight, Kev."

"Got home early. Dad, Mason's dirty."

"Did you check?" His dad sets down a knife.

"Listen to him." Kevin's dad shoots him a look.

So Kevin checks, and sure enough. Number two. "I'll do it." Thing is, Kevin didn't need to check. He could tell by the whimpers.

Kevin moves Mason to the floor and takes the diaper off. "How long's he been dirty like this, Dad?"

"Listen, Kev. I don't know. Your mom's at the store."

"You can tell by the way he was whimpering, Dad." His dad ignores him and grabs a glass of water.

When he finishes with the diaper, Kevin picks the baby up again. "Good news at work. I can help out a little more here at home. Then, yeah, I'm going back. But it's like a vacation today."

"Paid or unpaid?"

"Not paid, but—figured I'd help with Mason, and then go back. Maybe find another job. Maybe not."

Kevin's dad makes a sour face. "Uh, Kevin. The whole reason your mom and I are helping you is so you can apply to colleges, or find a long-term job, or you know, do something with your life. So, we aren't doing this forever. We need, more than you helping now, to make sure you're set up for later."

Kevin knows that's true, but his dad is also cranky. Really, he's been cranky since Mason came along, not like one of those happy grandfathers in the commercials, in a red plaid shirt with white hair, standing there, swinging the baby around or whatever. He's still young, he doesn't even have much gray yet. But he looks older than he did just a year ago, when he'd seemed invincible, when Kevin was finishing his senior year of high school and had to tell his dad that he felt lost, that Amber was pregnant, that she didn't want the baby, but he did, somehow he really did.

Kevin remembers telling Amber once, before she got pregnant, how babies all look alike. He still thinks that a little too, except Mason clearly has his face, the ears that stick out, poor bastard, fat cheeks and sunken eyes. If the ears don't stop him, and if his face turns out all right, if he gets a good jaw and gets tall and all that like Kevin, maybe he'll be a lady's man like Kevin was, at least before the baby. Or, maybe Kevin's just wrong about that. Maybe he doesn't know what a lady's man is. After all, he couldn't keep Amber.

He loved her. He really did. First, he loved watching her kick up those cowboy boots on the high school drill team. Then, at some point, he loved all of her. He loved watching TV with her, he loved her surprisingly loud laugh. None of that changed when her belly started getting bigger. And, as he told her, he didn't understand it, but he wanted this stupid baby and this stupid life together and stupid you.

"And you'll let me do all the work, won't you?" she'd said. "And my life will be all gone." But he'd badgered her so much, convinced her finally, went to every appointment with her, and she'd finally come around.

"You'll fall in love with him once you see him," Kevin had promised her, but she hadn't. Not even close. It turned out he was the stupid one.

"So Kevin," his dad is saying between bites of sandwich. "This is your full-time job now? Staying home, so you can listen to different kinds of baby cries?"

Kevin throws his hands up in the air. "What the hell, dad?" He takes the baby, storms off into his childhood bedroom, and waits there with the door closed.

When he hears his mother come home, he comes out. He puts Mason down and helps her carry in the groceries from her car and then put them away.

"Dad doesn't do much," Kevin says. His dad is out of earshot in another room. "Was he the same when I was a baby?"

She thinks for a moment. "Yeah, about the same."

Mason makes some fussing noises. "I'll bet he's a hungry boy," Kevin's mother says. "Does he want a bottle?"

"A boy," Kevin repeats. "You wouldn't really know by the sound."

His mother laughs. "Why do you think you'd be able to tell?"

"Oh, I don't know." Kevin blushes and feels stupid that he'd thought that boys wouldn't cry the same. Or that they'd sound a little less—desperate. Yes, that's what the sound is like to him, desperate for everything.

Kevin thinks back and can't remember ever seeing his dad cry, or any man in his family. Not once. When Kevin's dad is sad or angry, he disappears. He goes into the garage and fiddles with things. The car, a piece of wood that needs sanding, anything. He gets a stain on his shirt, a splinter in his hand. Maybe his tears are actually splinters. Maybe he cries with his hands.

When Kevin told his dad about Amber and the baby, and his dad saw the reddening of Kevin's nose and eyes, the beginning of what might've been a cry, if Kevin had ever let it, his dad had turned away in embarrassment. Or maybe disgust.

With the bottle from Kevin's mother, the baby stops crying.

"Your dad says something happened at work."

"My boss let me go home early."

"Let you? Or told you? Were you being an ass to the customers?" His mother smiles when she asks.

"I was an ass. It's the truth. But, well, no, I didn't have a good reason. But—you know what? Regina likes me. I don't know why, but she does."

Kevin takes Mason from his mother and pinches the baby's arm in the process. Mason gives a high-pitched scream. "Sorry, little guy. Sorry, sorry," Kevin says. Not a girl cry or a boy cry but an animalistic cry, so high and primal Kevin feels it might break him wide open. Kevin pulls the baby toward his chest. He is surprised by his own tenderness.

Kevin wonders what kind of husband he would've been. He was actually looking forward to doing stupid things like grocery trips and going out to restaurants with Amber and Mason, and cleaning up their dishes after dinner, and then, he doesn't know, making love and kissing the baby, and the whole stupid life he thought they were going to have.

"I've decided to go for full custody," Kevin says to his mom. He decides like that, just in that moment. Or, rather, he decided earlier today, on the phone call, when he imagined Amber in the two-seater, riding across Florida fancy-free.

But it's not just that. He wants Mason all the time. Mason steadies him. And, he thinks—so far, anyway—he steadies Mason. He doesn't want him with Amber, a mother prone to coldness. Even before the baby, she would get mad at Kevin sometimes for little things, freeze up and give him the silent treatment. She could be cruel. But she knew that about herself.

"I don't have the maternal instinct," she'd told him when they'd first learned about the pregnancy.

"You will," Kevin had insisted. "Women always do when the baby comes." But he was wrong, stupid wrong.

Kevin rocks Mason in his arms. Mason's head flops around until Kevin steadies it with a palm.

"Does Amber want custody?" his mom asks as she puts the last box of cereal into a cabinet.

"What does Amber think? Geez mom, I don't know. Maybe I would if she would ever answer her phone. Or any texts."

An image shoots into Kevin's mind just then. Amber, who wanted to be a professional dancer, still tiny, and all belly, getting bigger and bigger. In the last few months, she wasn't herself at all. She just looked—scared.

"She just drove off," his mom says in a musing way. Not severe enough for Kevin's taste.

"Was I like this as a baby, Mom? Like—this little?"

She nods absently. Now Kevin wants to know how his dad felt about him when he was a tiny thing who could barely steady his head. Because if Kevin didn't start out kind of numb, if he wasn't always this way, he must've gotten here somehow.

He needs a distraction from all this thinking. Kevin texts Hannah. He tells her he's not sure about this job, and she texts back a broken heart. Kevin tries not to read too much into it. Then he feels a little wave of panic that he won't see her again. He texts, *Want to come over and watch a basketball game tonight?*

At yr parents? Duuude.

And then another. *Jk Kev. Sounds fun.*

Hannah didn't date in high school. Kevin's not even sure whether she likes men, let alone him, but he does like being around her. He'll make some dip, and they'll hang out this evening, and his parents will have to be normal for a little while because she's there. It's not Amber, but,

Kevin thinks, you know what? Amber didn't even like basketball. She didn't even like sports. Kevin is going to teach Mason to love basketball. And he's going to be a Wizards fan. Oh, shit yeah. And root against Orlando Magic. Miami Heat too. Kevin will be a good dad, not a perfect one. Hell, Mason will root against anyone from Florida. Kevin feels happy now at the thought.

Hannah texts again. *Maybe the call center isn't right for you.* Kevin's stomach drops again. He imagines living with his parents forever. He is about to fire off something back, something mildly insulting, when he sees the three little dots pop up on his phone. He steadies himself and waits. Then she texts, *They have an opening in one of the lots. In person.* And then, after a minute, *I'd miss working with you oc.*

Kevin's glad he took a beat before responding. He's trying to do that more. He thinks about it for another minute. Headphones off. Face-to-face. He'd miss Hannah too. But—off screens, into the real world. It feels like the right next step.

He texts back. *Hmmm. Maybe I'd like that. I'd miss u 2.*

He gets off the phone and tells his mom what he's thinking about.

"Good. Maybe a change would be a blessing," his mom says. "Think about what's coming next."

"Yeah, a lot of people take a gap year, so that's what I'm doing, don't worry. I'll get to next steps."

Kevin likes the look of relief on his mom's face. He decides to tell his dad too.

Kevin looks for his dad and finds him in the garage. He remembers following his dad all around the house as a kid, talking to him. Room to room. How long has his dad been walking away from him, and Kevin going after him? Kevin thinks maybe this is just how it's always been for him. Just follow the person around, hoping they'll love you. Well, he sure as hell isn't following anyone to Tampa.

Kevin's dad is sitting on a garage stool, staring off. "They might want me on site, at one of the lots. And I'm going to have a friend over this evening," Kevin says. "To watch a game." He wants his dad to see how his life is going to come together. Kevin left the door open, and Mason starts crying again from somewhere inside.

"Will you? Will someone?" his dad says. He squints his eyes shut, trying to block out the sound. Instead, the wails grow louder.

Did Kevin sound that way as a baby? Did his dad take pity on him? Did he not hear the crying? Or, did he hear it and hate it? Kevin's mom is in the bathroom, so Kevin grabs Mason and tries to soothe him.

"Dad," Kevin says, returning to the garage with Mason. His voice cracks as it strains to overcome the cries. The garage smells of gasoline and oil. There is no need for his dad to check out the car, Kevin knows. The engine's been messed up for months. What's he looking at out here? "Dad. Did you hear me? What I said about the job?"

"Can't even—have a conversation. Will someone please shut that baby up!" his dad yells.

"No!" Kevin bangs his hand on the hood of his dad's messed up Honda, startling Mason, sending him into shrieks. "I'm going to let him cry. I'm going to go for a promotion. And I'm having a girl over to watch basketball tonight. But first, I'm going to let this baby cry as much as he wants. It's his right."

Kevin feels a welling up inside him too, but then it goes back down again. Where did his tears go? They're not like Mason's big, fat, wet ones, rolling down his face. They've got to end up somewhere. Maybe they're lost somewhere far away, just like Amber. Rolling down the highway in style, maybe in a Porsche Boxster, going on and on and on.

Plastic Teeth

"Give me your teeth," Mom says. Grandma ignores her, leans on an elbow tucked in the tray of her wheelchair, and stares at a calendar on the wall. It's turned to August, a picture of Paris, although we live in Tennessee and none of us has been farther than New York City.

"I'm eighty years old. I'll do as I like," Grandma says. We're in a small room with one window and barely space to stretch our arms. Grandma's hair is in loose white curls and smells of hairspray. She wears a pearl necklace, like a Hollywood starlet. I've seen pictures from when she was my age, nineteen, in teetering heels and dark, glossy lipstick. I'm not surprised my grandfather asked her to marry him the week they met, although she made him wait a year. Mom told me once Grandma had the highest grades in her high school and that every boy was in love with her.

"Mom, do you want me to clean your teeth?" The nursing home is supposed to clean Grandma's dentures, but nothing happens with any consistency unless Mom is around. Mom, the youngest of four and herself a mother of four, brings the brisk efficiency of a large household to everything she does.

My mother is beautiful, too, but she downplays it, wearing shapeless blazers, keeping her blonde hair tucked into a bun. My taste leans closer to Grandma's.

I'm in town for spring break. My college friends are off to Europe, but I'm visiting my boyfriend, Josh—a curly-haired man with laughing eyes who makes me forget everything else. We've been dating since our senior year of high school—for more than a year.

"Dentures," Mom says. She's trying not to look rushed, but I know she has to get back to work. She is all movement in my mind. "You need your right hand."

Grandma smiles wryly. "What were we talking about?"

Mom leans toward me. "She does this all the time. Thinks she's funny. Mom. I'm not forgetting what we're doing."

Grandma sighs toward the calendar. "I always wanted to see Paris."

In the picture, a boardwalk lines a blue-gray stretch of water. Josh doesn't want to travel any farther than the nearest movie theater. I promise myself I'll travel someday, with or without him. I'm not going to waste another spring break at home.

"Do you want gum disease?" Mom glances at her watch.

Grandma shakes her head. "Your mother was actually very good when she was a little girl. She didn't turn stubborn until she started dating."

"Mom, I told you. You can't distract—not funny," Mom says, her mouth turning down to stifle a laugh. But when Mom looks at me, her shoulders shake. It breaks through. We laugh until the tears come. Grandma is pleased.

"Would you bring me some water?" Grandma asks.

"Okay. You win," Mom says. "But when I get back, I want those dentures." She whispers to me, "This is what my life is like."

When Mom leaves for the cafeteria, I see my chance.

"How was Mom stubborn?" I ask.

Grandma smiles, because she has an ally now. "Too ready to marry." Her words are slurred, so I lean in. "Married at nineteen! And pregnant a year later."

I try to imagine Mom at my age, but I can't. If she has any life regrets, she hasn't shared them. She is not a romantic like Grandma. But I think she finds pleasure in the little things she allows herself—a movie night in, dinner with Dad at the steakhouse where Josh works.

Josh is supposed to be saving for an apartment, but it never amounts to much. He was supposed to go to college like me but decided to work a year first, and then missed the deadline to apply. I think about Mom and promise myself I won't get married or pregnant for a long time. I can be stubborn too.

Mom returns with a glass of water for Grandma. "Mom, give me your dentures. *No*, Mom. Put down your cup. You need your right hand free."

"I'll use my left," Grandma says. "Bossy, bossy."

"You can't, Mom. Put the cup down. You can't use that hand."

"I'll show you."

"No."

"You just watch."

Mom bows her head. "Okay," she says. "Use your left hand. Show me." The room seems to freeze, and I suddenly become aware of the sun shining through the window, forming a hot square of light on my neck.

"Your left side is paralyzed, Mom. You can't move it." Mom's eyes redden.

"I'll hold the cup, Grandma," I say. Grandma finally takes her dentures out with her right hand and puts them on her tray. She looks away so she doesn't have to see them.

When Mom slips away to brush Grandma's teeth, I want to tell Grandma something happy. I tell her I think Josh and I are in love. She sets her jaw, and I wonder if she heard me. I follow her eyes to the calendar. When I see the picture of Paris, I feel stupid for making a promise to myself I don't know I can keep.

I have a suspicion Josh is saving for a ring. He told me once he didn't want to lose me to one of those college guys.

Mom is running water in the bathroom. "Don't marry right away," Grandma says over the sound.

"See the world first," Grandma says, stretching forward the arm she can. I don't know what to say.

Suddenly, I see Grandma and Mom and all the women I can imagine in my family, all way back, pushing the only levers they have at any given time. Make him wait. No, I'll marry now. Give me your teeth. I'll keep them in my mouth, thank you.

When Mom comes out of the bathroom with Grandma's teeth, I don't look at her. Instead, I imagine Grandma at nineteen, in heels on cobblestone. I imagine her with loose curls, a sly look, painted lips, in Paris. I imagine her and me together, both of us nineteen, sipping champagne, eating breadsticks and olives. When she asks for another glass, I wonder aloud if we should really order another, and she says, "I'll do as I like."

Room for Three

Amy's eyes rested on pink walls, the color of raw beef. Parnell and Patterson: famously, a meat grinder of a New York law firm. Noelle, the managing partner, sat at the head of a table that smelled of lemon polish. She wore a headband across the top of her head like a tiara.

Noelle had just asked Amy a question: Would she defend the makers of Zorpitose? Amy considered Noelle's question and touched a black earring dangling from her ear. The anti-nausea drug did a host of things, supposedly, but Amy was a lawyer, not a scientist.

The truth was that joining the case could be good for her. Noelle had already made partner by thirty-five, Amy's age. Most of the other partners were men. There must have been something remarkable about Noelle, though Amy couldn't put her finger on it. She rubbed at her earring again—black onyx.

At Amy's elementary school, there was a plastic slide under the hot Texas sun and a small wooden fort on the playground. It looked like a palace, with a long ladder and a moat of pebbles all the way around. She had tried, only once her entire fourth-grade year, to climb to the top, where Bridget and her two best friends sat every recess.

Amy was only a few rungs up when she saw Bridget's face peering down. Bridget styled her blonde hair in a hairspray-coated poof at her forehead. It was just starting to drizzle outside, and raindrops hung on Bridget's bangs like jewels. The rest of her wavy hair splayed around her shoulders. She had blue eyes and a constellation of freckles across her delicate nose.

"There's only room for three," Bridget said. Next to Bridget, Jane wore her brown hair in a high ponytail with two scrunchies, and Kira, the shortest of the three, tugged on a lock of stick-straight red hair and looked sorry.

Amy climbed down and left the fort. Looking back over her shoulder, she noticed the girls had their backpacks spread out around them. What Bridget had said wasn't true. The fort could have held five or even six girls if they'd wanted.

At lunchtime, Bridget and Jane and Kira sat together again. Amy sat with her own friends, a girl she'd known since the second grade and another girl who loved playing pretend.

When she told the story of the fort, she did it to make them laugh. For her Jane impression, she tugged at her ponytail and pursed her lips. To do Kira, she watched the other girls and laughed at whatever they said. Imitating Bridget was the hardest. It was a blank smile, without blinking. But it made her friends laugh hardest of all.

Amy was good at the impressions because she watched the girls in the fort so closely—the way they spoke, their clothes, their hair. She'd concluded that what separated her from Bridget and Bridget's friends was her own hair—thin, brown, and curly. With some effort, Amy could cinch it into a ponytail like Jane's. It took half the morning and a cloud of hairspray to straighten out the top, and even after that, what remained coiled and sprang vengefully in every direction.

Amy's mother would say the problem was not her hair and that the other girls would be lucky to have a friend like Amy, who was loyal and kind. But Amy knew it *was* about the hair, and also the way Amy excelled at math and nearly everything in school. And the girls weren't looking for someone loyal and kind, and it had been many years since her mother was in school.

So Amy did not share with her mother the real reason she wanted to be invited into the fort, which was to catch the attention of Layne, a boy who loved drawing, stood inches above the other boys, and more often than not was king at four square. She wasn't sure how exactly she would catch his attention, except that all the boys seemed to love the girls in the fort.

In class, Amy watched Layne filling his notebooks with sketches of video game characters. Her one real interaction with him was the time a kickball came her way in gym class, ricocheting off the side of her face, and Layne ran over to ask if she was all right. He dressed in all black and had shaggy brown hair. As he was walking away, he whispered, "I hate PE," which was the bravest thing Amy had ever heard a boy say.

After the morning associates' meeting, Noelle's secretary, Linda, came into Amy's office, leaning heavily on a cane. She closed the door behind her and flopped into a chair.

"I'm afraid I said too much this time." Linda played with a tassel on her blouse. "I told Noelle what I thought about the class action. We shouldn't get involved in this one. I think you agree."

"I didn't say that. I said I wanted to think about it," Amy said.

Linda shrugged her shoulders and settled deeper into the chair. Amy checked her watch. Linda was an odd one. She held long, frequent phone calls with her adult son, Billy, reminding him to pay his bills and take his medicine. Some of the associates exchanged amused smiles while Linda talked. But because she'd been at the firm longer than anyone else, even Noelle, Linda was afforded certain privileges, like the loud phone calls. Linda moaned into her hands. "I'm afraid I'll be fired now."

"You're overreacting."

"People aren't as nice as you think." Linda regarded Amy a moment. "Billy needs me. I need this job. But still—I have a conscience. I had to say something."

"You didn't have to."

Linda sighed. "Have you heard what the stuff can do? The side effects? Vision problems? Headaches?" She lowered her voice, "Other things? Well, anything for pregnant women, you can't be too careful. I'd hate to think—"

"It's just an anti-nausea," Amy said, feeling annoyed.

"Maybe so." Linda put down the tassel of her blouse. "I think I'll stay. But if Noelle turns on me—"

"She wouldn't."

"If she does—it would be good to have someone in my corner."

Amy nodded. That seemed to satisfy Linda. "Watch out for yourself too," Linda said. "Sharp elbows this time of year."

It was true. Three partners were rumored to be on their way out this year, leaving space for three senior associates to move up after December. Although no one knew exactly who they would be, everyone agreed there would be only three new partners, and probably only one, if any, would be a woman. Linda sighed and shifted in her chair. "Hailey told Noelle you're not partner material." Hailey was another senior associate Amy suspected might make partner before she did.

"She what?"

"I think the exact phrase was *in over her head*." Linda gave a knowing smile. "I've seen this play out a million times. There's no prize for being nice."

In the first month of the fifth grade, their last year before middle school, Kira invited all seven girls in their new class over for a slumber party. On a leather couch with white fuzz coming out of the lining, they talked about what they'd done over the summer. Bridget and Jane had gone to camp, where they swam, rode horses, and met boys. There was a new girl at the sleepover, Carly, who was slender and athletic, and who'd gone to the same camp. Kira, like Amy, had stayed home and gone to the local pool.

"I saw Layne at the pool," Kira said, tugging at her red hair. "In his swimsuit." She giggled. Amy had seen him too, towering over the other boys their age, swimming confidently. He could have passed for a boy already in middle school.

Bridget's eyes widened just for a moment. "I barely thought about Layne all summer," she said. She turned to Kira. "What did you talk about?"

"Nothing," Kira said, shifting in her seat. "We stood in line at the vending machine. But then, he bought me a bag of Doritos." Amy thought she saw Bridget stiffen at that.

The girls listened to Ace of Base, which Bridget had just discovered. "I saw the sign," Bridget sang, holding up a spoon to her chin. She leaned toward Kira, crooning, "How can a person like me care for you?" Kira giggled nervously and stared at her shoes.

After dinner, they tried to give Amy a makeover. While Amy sat in front of a mirror in Kira's bedroom, Kira and Jane fussed with Amy's brown curls. Bridget and the other girls tried on their own makeup they'd brought in plastic Caboodles.

"When you brush it, it just gets bigger," Kira said.

"You shouldn't brush it," Amy protested. Kira dug in with a rolled brush.

"She should grow it longer," Jane said.

"It doesn't get longer, just curlier," Amy said.

"Too curly. That's the problem," Bridget said, looking up from her purple Caboodle.

They brushed and sprayed and made Amy's hair wild, until finally, defeated, they declared nothing could be done.

Kira's house was in an older part of the city, with small, dark houses. Jane and Bridget exchanged a look when Kira's dad passed by and settled in front of the living room TV. He had a mustache, a cigarette, and a belly that spilled out over his pants. Everything in Kira's house smelled of smoke and TV dinners.

In the morning at breakfast, Bridget opened a carton of milk and took a dramatic whiff before pouring it onto her cereal. Jane made a face. Kira pretended not to see it, and Amy watched the other girls gawk at the scene like vultures over a sick animal.

The following Monday at recess, when Kira went to climb the long ladder leading up to the fort, Amy noticed the third position was already occupied by Carly.

Kira fought tears through the rest of recess and had only Amy to comfort her. Her exile from the fort was whispered and repeated in bathrooms and hallways, giving pleasure to the girls who'd never once been in the fort at recess.

Kira had worn a T-shirt with a scrunchie tied to the side that day, and Bridget declared after recess that only babies did that. Kira never wore her shirts like that again and stopped talking so much in class.

The following morning, Linda surprised everyone by calling in sick before a meeting with the clients from the pharmaceutical company that produced Zorpitose. The other secretaries were occupied, and there wasn't time to call in a temp. On top of that, they'd had to change rooms at the last minute because of a mix-up in reservations.

Amy tried to catch up with Noelle and Hailey, who were always speed walking together. Right after they rounded the corner and disappeared, a man's voice called out, "Where am I supposed to go?" and Amy met him at Linda's desk.

She remembered his voice from a conference call. He looked to be in his fifties and smelled of cologne. He glanced at the nameplate at the desk. "Linda? Where's the meeting with Noelle? I thought it was the main conference room."

"I'm Amy. They moved down the hall."

He gave a curious smile. "Amy. You're not Linda? Are you a first-year?"

"Senior associate."

He cocked his head. "You can't be more than what, twenty-five?"

"Add a decade."

"Honestly? I don't believe it."

She smiled in a way she'd mastered years ago when she'd worked in college as a bartender, quickly, with nothing in the eyes. It was the desk, she thought. He'd never have said that if she hadn't met him at Linda's desk.

"That way," Amy said. She pointed down the hallway.

"Why didn't anyone tell me the room moved?"

"Hailey's the lead associate on the case," Amy said.

"So *she* forgot to tell me."

Amy considered that. "It wouldn't surprise me. She forgets things sometimes."

He raised an eyebrow. "Sometimes?"

Amy gave a knowing shrug.

The man exhaled and shifted his weight from one leg to the other. "Are there others on the case?"

"Plenty of others."

As the man disappeared down the hallway, Amy looked down at Linda's desk. All across it were overly sentimental pictures of a gray cat and of her son, Billy. He appeared to be about twenty, with big cheeks and squinty eyes. He was an overgrown boy, with a face that was sweet and yet not altogether present. There were five pictures of Billy, as many as the cat—Billy on a fishing boat holding up his catch, Billy at a water park, Linda and Billy together. Linda's little shrine to Billy and the cat.

Amy never fit in with Bridget and her friends, but over the fifth grade, she built up her own circle. At recess, while the athletic girls played and the pretty girls ruled the fort, they went on long walks through the soccer fields, talking. There were days when Amy didn't think of the fort at all.

It was well known that Bridget, Jane, and Carly would have a pool party at Bridget's house to celebrate the end of the fifth grade, which was also the end of elementary school. Amy knew she wouldn't make the list of invitees, but she was organizing her own celebration with two of her friends.

When Amy invited them, she presented each with a different stone. They pretended the rocks had magical powers and held them every day at recess as they discussed their plans. On the Saturday after the last day of school, they would meet at Amy's house, spend all day in the forest, and then spend the night at her house.

One day at recess, just before the end of the school year, Layne saw the stones and asked Amy about them. She told him what they were planning and watched his mouth curl into a smile.

"There's a tire swing," she explained. "I found it once in the woods, hanging from a tree over a creek, next to an abandoned tree house. It's completely hidden from the road."

"Your *own* fort," he said, shaking his head in wonder. And Amy realized she *had* discovered her own place, hidden behind the leaves. "Sounds cooler than that thing," Layne said, gesturing toward the wooden fort where the three girls sat watching them.

Amy had never considered that. Next year, they would all be in middle school and leave all of this behind. And it struck her what the fort really was—not a palace, just a piece of a wooden playground for babies. Why hadn't she understood any of this before?

"We're going to spend the whole day in the tree house with our stones," Amy said. Then her face flushed. It was the sort of thing Bridget and the other girls would laugh at. But Layne didn't laugh.

"I have a rock polisher," he said.

"Awesome." Amy rubbed a stone in her hand.

The next week at recess, Layne approached Amy again and pulled from his pocket a set of earrings.

"I have something for you. Black onyx," he said.

"Oh." She leaned in for a closer look. "Did you make them?"

"I polished and set the stones myself. It's for you. More magic stones."

She took them in her shaking hands. The settings were silver in color, weighing almost nothing. The rocks had been glued to the settings, and they were spectacular—black, smooth, and iridescent.

She rubbed the polished stones with her thumb and marveled at how the black sparkled in the sunlight. "You *are* an artist."

Amy glanced up at the fort to see three pairs of eyes watching her. She looked back down immediately, heart pounding.

"Oh. Your ears are pierced, right?" Layne asked, leaning in close to see.

Amy nodded. She could feel his breath on her. Her feet felt heavy and stuck to the blacktop. She could hardly speak.

~

At the morning associates' meeting the following week, Hailey forgot her notes. When Noelle zeroed in on a question from a client, Hailey hesitated and offered to check.

"That won't be necessary," Noelle said, smoothing her hair. "Let's have Meaghan take on this next memo." Meaghan, another senior associate, smiled and touched a silk scarf at her neck. She wore a scarf nearly every day and tied them into intricate knots, the way Amy imagined you'd learn to do if you'd gone to private school in the Northeast like Meaghan had.

Noelle turned toward Hailey, tapping her fingers on the table. Amy's eyes rested on the pink walls as she remembered her encounter with the client. After the previous week's meeting, he had told Noelle he'd prefer to work with a different associate. Hailey had fallen out of favor after that, and Noelle's ire now seemed to follow her everywhere. Hailey's emails suddenly weren't good enough. Her memos were riddled with mistakes.

And like magic, Amy was in Noelle's good graces. Amy had even begun to imitate how the others spoke, quickly and without emotion, always certain. She felt she was becoming smarter and better at her job. She'd finally begun to understand you had to take cases like this from time to time and told Noelle she would be glad to join the team. When she was partner, she'd take on only the cases she wanted. But for now, she could do this.

After the meeting, Meaghan came up to Amy and eyed her earrings.

"I like them," she said. "They look vintage." She caught Hailey watching them. "You should come to happy hour with us tomorrow," Meaghan said to Amy. "A few of us go on Fridays."

As everyone filed out of the conference room, Hailey sped off to her office, and Amy noticed a strange look among the others. One associate curled up his lip. Meaghan gave a little smile and looked down. It was the quickest of exchanges. Amy had seen that look somewhere before. Her mind flashed back to that moment many years ago—a quick look shared over a milk carton, then a casting out, a shift in the order of things.

Later that evening, Amy signed into Facebook and looked up Layne. They had connected as friends in college, and she'd seen his posts from time to time but not recently. Now she saw he was a tall, refined version of himself. He'd founded an accounting company. There was no sign that he still drew.

He'd married Bridget, who looked the same as always—a pink smile, blonde hair, with professionally done pictures of their children. They had a baby girl wrapped in a pink blanket, a boy starting to walk, another girl who was already starting to look just like Bridget, with striking blue eyes and freckles across her nose.

On a whim, Amy sent a private message to Layne. "Found some old jewelry today. Black onyx. Reminded me of you." It was a lie, of course. Over the years, she'd barely let the earrings out of her sight.

An hour later, he replied. "Why? Maybe I'm dense."

Of course he hadn't remembered. Why had she assumed he would? Her face felt hot.

She typed back, "I think you gave them to me in elementary. When you were into polishing rocks."

He responded. "Oh yeah! God, I was a nerd."

After dinner in front of the TV, Amy checked Facebook again. There was another message from Layne. "Did you know in ancient times, onyx was supposed to protect you from your enemies?"

She smiled and waited an hour to respond. "It didn't work."

He wrote back immediately. "Too bad. At least you still look good."

Amy's heart pounded. She shut her computer without responding. As she lay in bed that night, she remembered something about the case: It was true that the plaintiffs seemed to have strong evidence that they'd suffered from the drug. She wished she hadn't heard that or that she could forget it. It did trouble her. But then, it wasn't solid proof. Health impacts were difficult to prove. Amy had found some good research for their client. Noelle would be pleased with that. Then Amy's thoughts returned to Layne.

In middle school, there was no playground and no fort, but there were other coveted statuses—spots at lunch tables, get-togethers on weekends. Amy began to form new friendships, but from time to time still watched the other girls with a pang.

In high school, she joined the debate team and learned to argue. She found that she loved to read history and learned the power of her own convictions. She began to suspect she might leave Dallas altogether and study somewhere else. She thought she might want to be a lawyer.

Layne and Bridget began dating. It was only natural, Amy thought, as they both rose to the top of the school's social circles. Amy felt a pang of disappointment that Layne had fallen in with the popular crowd of athletes and cheerleaders in high school but hoped it wouldn't last, that eventually he'd long for her the way she always had for him.

She kept the earrings, because she loved the way they made her feel. They reminded her of the afternoon in the woods with her friends and recreating herself, that the world was so much bigger than Bridget and her circle of girls.

On Friday, Amy went with Meaghan and three other women senior associates from the office to a cocktail bar. Amy asked whether Hailey was joining, and Meaghan said she'd forgotten to invite her. Amy ordered a wine. The bar was bright and warm, and a light rain was visible through a window. As the wind picked up and the people outside clutched their scarves and coats, Amy finished her wine and ordered a hot cider. As the second round started, the gossip grew edgier and turned to the question of who might make partner next.

"Does anyone here know how Noelle made partner?" Meaghan asked, touching her fingertips together. "Linda told me years ago." She paused until the others egged her on. "One of her rivals was slated to be picked. But she managed to convince his client he'd been overbilling. The client requested to work with her. That's how she got the big pharma account."

The others exchanged looks of disapproval, jealousy, and awe.

"Linda talks too much," one said. "That's probably what got her fired."

Linda had thirty days to find another job. The official reason was that she'd taken excessive leave without requesting it in advance. But that had never been a problem for her before. No one believed it was the real reason she was being let go, but no one pressed the issue either.

"Linda does talk too much. Why do you think Noelle wanted her out?" Meaghan asked in a quiet voice. Amy thought of those pictures of Billy, his squinty eyes, and Linda wanting to take care of him. She suspected there was another reason. It wasn't just the gossip. It was that she made Noelle think about things she didn't want to. She'd protested the pharma case.

The women began to dissect the week's associates' meeting. Amy still remembered Hailey's comment that she, Amy, wasn't partner material, and the way she'd never mentioned the happy hours before. And then one of the women brought up the way Hailey had flubbed the last associates' meeting.

Amy blurted out, in a perfect imitation of Hailey, what she'd said that very afternoon, adding a slight southern drawl, "Well, I left my notes in the office. I didn't knoooow this would come up." Amy wondered if she'd gone too far.

The others looked shocked, until Meaghan cracked a smile, her shoulders shook, and then the others joined in the laughter. Meaghan's upper lip curled, revealing bright white teeth and pink gums.

"I doubt Hailey will make partner," Meaghan said, tugging at her scarf. "But I'll bet most of us do eventually."

Amy's heart pounded, and she felt flooded with warmth and acceptance. She knew how easily Noelle and Meaghan got along and how much easier it would be at the firm to have Meaghan's support. Maybe Meaghan would make partner this year and Amy would next year. That would be all right.

Amy wondered what Hailey was doing and remembered Kira crying years ago, after she'd been banned from the fort. Her face had been red, ugly, and tear-stained. Amy had decided then that kind of crying was always ugly and she'd never do it publicly.

She remembered inviting Kira to spend the night and how eagerly Kira had accepted. Amy had mocked Bridget for Kira's benefit, laughing and baring her teeth like a fierce beauty queen. It had made Kira smile through her tears.

She knew what was coming for Hailey.

"Hailey's a bit—how shall I put it?" Meghan looked around, drawing out the moment.

"Dumb," Amy finished, and they laughed.

"I saw Linda in your office the other day," Meaghan said to Amy. "What was that about?"

Amy shrugged. She knew Linda's job was a lost cause. So she squinted her eyes the way Linda did when she was thinking. "Biiiiilly," she said. "Did ya pay the phone bill? Did ya?"

"Oh Lord, you sound just like her," Meaghan said.

"You should see her desk," Amy said, "Just Billy and the cat." It didn't feel right to say it, but she was able to put the feeling aside.

Meaghan leaned in toward Amy. "We do this every Friday. You should come out more."

Meaghan's brown hair fell in perfect waves over her shoulders. Amy decided then to get rid of her own curls and to do a blowout, with waves and highlights. She would transform herself. New York salons could make you into anyone.

And maybe it was time for a visit to Texas. She hadn't been back in years. She'd reach out to Layne, grab a drink with him. She would show up with new hair and the highlights, a tight dress, something that couldn't have been bought anywhere but New York. Bridget wouldn't have anything like that.

For just a moment, Amy wished for a forest full of magic, for magic stones she could wear in her ears and feel powerful, the way she had at the end of the fifth grade.

That day, in the woods, they'd pretended to be powerful goddesses who kept evil at bay. They held their magic stones, nibbled on wild onions, chased cottontails, and caught tadpoles in buckets.

Then they cleaned up, ate dinner, and stayed up for hours talking. It was the first time Amy could remember not wishing for anything, simply stretching out her legs and laughing until her sides hurt. But that was a pretend game for kids, and only children believed in magic.

Amy took a long swig of cider. Outside, the streets were slick with rain, reflecting Manhattan's streetlights and neon signs. It felt good to be warm and full of hot drink.

Why had she carried the onyx earrings for years, worn them through high school and college and beyond? Well, that was from another time. She would not wear the black onyx again. She would not think about the forest or Kira's ugly, tear-stained face.

Amy flipped her hair, the way Hailey did. Everyone around her laughed, and the sound echoed through the little bar, filling Amy with delight. Someone ordered bruschetta. Amy took a bite with such eagerness she bit her cheek and tasted blood.

She'd been climbing all this time, hadn't she? For the first time, she felt delightfully beautiful. The fort was so high up, higher than she had imagined it would be, and everyone below looked so small, and she knew everything would be so easy after this.

Dinnertime

The slicing comes easily, an elastic, watery quality like soft tofu. The knife moves to the cutting board, which you fill with bite-sized chunks. Your mind drifts backward. The experience is cathartic in a way, this non-use, or, rather, other use of your brain.

Your baby boy makes animal noises somewhere at your feet, while your daughter reads a book at the kitchen table. She is already reading two years ahead of schedule.

You too were years ahead from kindergarten on. You remember sitting at home while the boys played outside, doing your homework and thinking you were going to do something incredible with your life.

"Grrrr," the baby says. His eyes squint with merriment, surprised at the sounds he is making.

"That's right, a bear growls," you hear yourself say and wonder how it is that you can carry on entire conversations without thinking at all. Still, he must be getting something from the sound of your voice. His words are taking off.

You remember the first time you knew what you wanted out of life—to write a book of stories. You were just in middle school at the time, staring at pictures of the authors on your parents' books, and thinking, couldn't that be you?

Your daughter says something.

"That's great," you tell her.

"Are you listening?" she demands.

"Of course."

"What did I say?"

You play it back. "You were practicing rhymes."

"Yes," she says. Long and leaning over the table, she already looks like a little woman. She turns back to her book.

You are almost done cutting. Your fingertips are sore from gripping the handle of the knife. You ought to get it sharpened. You reposition the handle and push down.

When your husband texts on his way home, he asks whether you've read his article. You have. You clean your hands and send back some thoughts. You reply to a work email on your phone. You cut more pieces of meat.

Your daughter asks you for some rhymes. "Slice, dice," you say.

She shrieks. "I slice nice!"

Once the cutting board is filled, you lift and turn it sideways over the skillet to slide the pieces of meat in. The oil splatters when it hits, singeing your hands. You stir until the pieces have browned.

"Meow," the boy says.

"Meow, little one," you say. "Kitty bowl coming up."

The pieces aren't enough for the dinner bowls. "Oh," you say. You overestimated how much there was.

"I slice thrice," you say. "Here." You grab little browned pieces for the kids to snack on while they wait. They look so hungry.

"More, Mommy!" your daughter says.

"Moooo!" agrees the boy.

"Moooo! Moooo! Moooo!" they chant together, the boy imitating the girl, and the girl imitating the boy.

Your husband texts again. He wonders if you remembered to pick something up for dinner. You reply with a thumbs up.

When you first became pregnant, one of the men at your office joked that you would start forgetting things, but it was actually your best year. It wasn't that your work suffered much. You could always make a little more time for everyone by working harder.

In the early days after your first was born, you used to steal away to work on the book—short stories, of all things. As if there weren't enough waste already in the world. Why did you call it stealing away, even in your own mind? But that was how it felt, sneaking away for an hour, stealing time and pieces of yourself that didn't belong to you any longer. You are embarrassed by how often you think of the stories you haven't finished and don't tell anyone about it, not even your husband or closest friends.

It's not that they wouldn't support you. But when it came down to taking an hour here or there to write, there was never time. Of course, you could write after the appointment, after the report, after dinner, after bedtime. Sometimes you lied, snuck away under another pretext to write, but even that became tiring.

And then, after your second came along, this feeling began to come on, this ability to speak without thinking at all. The feeling of operating perfectly without your mind.

The kids look so small and hungry, and you turn toward the stove and peel open the front of your forehead. Your fingernails tear into the soft membrane inside your head. You grab another handful before it closes up again. No one notices. You cut it into pieces.

"I dice nice," you say.

You add it to the pan. The membranes sizzle under the heat.

You tear off piece after piece. But it still doesn't seem to be enough.

Your daughter stares at her book. "What else rhymes with nice?"

"Paradise," you call out.

And isn't it? Didn't you choose this life? Does the world need more stories, or does it need food to fill bellies? Your daughter gives a beatific smile. They're getting bigger, and so very smart. You do take pride in that.

When your husband gets home, he tells you your edits to his article were good.

"What did I say again?" you ask.

"You're joking." He rubs your back and holds his hand out for a piece.

You give a baffled smile. You can't, for the life of you, remember what his article was about. You can't remember what any of this is about. Surely it all has to mean something.

You give him a piece. You ought to say no, and sometimes you do, but they are all so hungry, waiting with their expectant faces. Perhaps it's their fault for asking so eagerly, for assuming you have infinite treasures to share, assuming it's in your nature because you are a mother. Perhaps it's your own fault for being too tired to keep fighting, for holding the skillet, for being so willing to dig into yourself.

"Mommy doesn't remember things," your daughter says.

Sometimes, you look back and wonder if any of this might've been different, if you hadn't given so much away. The extra drop-off for your husband. The late night for work. It's always a small thing. Just a few minutes. A sliver, a membrane.

If you kept a little more for yourself, everyone might be a little hungrier, but wouldn't they make out all right? How would it feel to see your life played out whole, instead of torn into pieces, wondering which pieces, if any, still belonged to you. Sometimes you ache for the memory of what it was like to apply your whole mind and body to something, anything.

You stretch your fingers, arcing them backward. They are stiff from the cutting.

Your husband plants a kiss right above your nose, on your forehead. "What's for dinner? Smells good."

You shake your head and shrug. "I'm so tired I can hardly remember my name."

"Mommy brain," he says with a silly face, making the little boy laugh.

Dreams of a Sleek, Gray Sofa with Tufted Cushions

Inside the man's apartment, off a highway with high billboards and cars that rumbled all night, was a creased, brown hippopotamus of a couch. June refrained from telling the man his couch was ugly because he'd spent so much money on it, and besides, her kids liked it. It had infinite folds and crevices where they left toy cars and Cheez-Its, board game pieces, and bits of late-night Oreos he let them have, which June said she didn't mind so much, because they were bonding, after all. The couch was covered in fur and smelled like the man's dog, a border collie mix who liked rolling in grass, who left black and white hairs all over June's leggings, and who stared longingly sometimes out of the high living room window.

June and the man had met when he stayed at her hotel a year ago, new to town and with a U-Haul. He'd walked right up to the front desk where she was working through a burrito between checking in guests, and asked whether she could come see why his room key wasn't working.

Now, they sat together on his couch—the man and June, her kids and his dog, toys and McDonald's wrappers—and watched television in the evenings. Some mornings, June caught a fleeting happy feeling when the light shone in, and he whistled while making pancakes for them, and the boys ran trucks along the floorboards.

June collected these moments like coins in a bank. Enough savored moments had to add up to something of a good life, even if it wasn't the one she'd planned. But what tugged at her was this: the couch they sat on, rumpled, soft, uninspired fabric, while dreaming of other, better furniture where they could be sitting. Firmer cushions, sturdier wood, maybe something that twisted or had a floral design like the hotel chairs, somewhere beyond this in-between place she had accommodated herself to.

June had told the man recently she'd had a dream that was coming back to her in pieces, about her next place: a hip little sunlit house decorated like the hotel rooms, a faux animal rug, a tropical plant, the rest of it she couldn't yet recall, aside from the bright and happy feel of it. He said that sounded like a dream for twenty-year-olds, and neither of them were in their twenties any longer. He paused and didn't finish what he was going to say next, which June gathered had something to do with her wrinkled shirt, her loose-fitting jeans, her tennis shoes that had seen better days. Then the man asked if he was in the dream, and June said it was hard to remember.

He wasn't ever planning to go back home to Wyoming, but he missed empty spaces. He'd moved into the apartment not far from the hotel, and then put above the brown couch a painting of a man and horse on the open plains, the kind of art you might find in a hotel room, and she caught both him and the dog staring at it sometimes from the kitchen table. June reminded him sometimes, in moments like this, how happy they were together.

June said when she and the boys moved in completely, maybe the couch could go in another room. But he told her he liked it in the main room. He'd bought the couch after things ended with him and his wife, and it meant something to him, something about independence. Besides, he said, while sitting on the couch, legs up on the folding footrest June hated, that wasn't the point. What he'd meant to say earlier but hadn't was that the problem was the boys' stuff everywhere, poking into everything when they tried to sit, that it was too many toys and not enough space.

June stared at the dog hair on the rug at her feet and wondered who would blink first and vacuum it up. Probably her. Maybe after her next shift. Sometimes, when June worked the front desk, she watched the travelers rushing around with their suitcases and wondered what made them all come and go in such a hurry.

While the man lit a cigarette, June said she'd never gotten to pick a new sofa or chairs before. But that was a lie: she'd picked them out plenty of times over the years from the rolled-up furniture catalogs that came to her at the hotel. It wasn't the only lie, either. June had told him once she liked the couch, and it was too late to take back. There was something about the first lie that made it easier to spin another and another. Like how happy she was here. How she didn't have any plans to leave. June thought about that and stared up at the painting of the plains while the man took a drag. Then she closed her eyes and listened for the cars outside to pass. She made the brown couch vanish in her mind, with the crumbs and dog hair and everything else, until the apartment emptied out completely. And in its hollow place, she could almost feel the touch of fur at her feet, soft leather against her back.

Manna

When Caleb and his mom and sister leave in the morning for Easter Mass, it's pouring rain. Rain sloshing up to the ankles of Caleb's red rain boots. This is how it is in the Arizona desert. Nothing for weeks, then the sky opens up for days. Caleb wonders how his dad will find his way home through it all. He's been gone more than a month.

It started raining last night, was coming down in sheets by late morning. Caleb, seven, loves the rain soaking into earth, the smell of dust when the water droplets sizzle on the pavement. It's spectacular what can grow out here with so little. His dad used to take him and his sister Eliza to hike around Lake Havasu, where brown rocks rise up and palm trees ring the lake. Sometimes he'd stay with them and their mom for a week or two, once for a month. But then, like a cycle of nature, the hikes slow, his dad disappears in the evenings, comes home after Caleb's bedtime, slurring, rustling for food in the kitchen. His mom loses patience and kicks him out. Then he gets better and stays that way for a long time. Dry, dry, dry.

The last time he disappeared, Caleb's dad left a bag of gummies on Caleb's pillow with a note that promised he'd return by Easter. Caleb hid the gummies in his sock drawer and savors them, drawing one a day to make them last.

On the walk into church, Caleb spots a small, feathered animal on its side, black chin, eyes closed, little toes clenched—a dead quail. Eliza says it's a sparrow, but she's wrong. When they argue, their mother shushes them, grips Caleb's wrist, and leads them inside to the back pew.

Caleb is not sure whether he believes in prayer. But he likes the quiet, the candles and incense, watching his sister, eyes closed, lips moving. His mother is always asking him to stop telling stories that aren't true, but she seems to like the stories at Mass.

Afterward, as they rush through the rain to the car, Caleb is shocked to see the quail he was sure was dead isn't hurt at all. The spot where the bird lay is gone. He finds it preening under a bush.

He points to the bird, finger quivering. Eliza says it's not the same one, but she's wrong again. It doesn't matter that Caleb isn't sure whether quail really do rise from the dead. Happy tears gather in Caleb's eyes. The bird flies to a nearby tree, a flash of brown against the gray, drizzled sky. A black feathered crown sits atop its head, as it gazes down on them.

They're going to hunt for eggs at home in the afternoon. Caleb doesn't say it, but he wants to wait a little longer for his dad. No one has said Caleb's dad is returning today, but he remembers. He hopes his dad can see the roads all right, wipers swooshing through the rain. Caleb knows that soon, he will appear, dripping wet, carrying a duffel bag. He'll say he's sorry he's been so lost wandering through the desert, trying to get home.

What will happen next, only Caleb knows. When they sit down for lunch, Caleb's dad will point outside. The rain will die down to a pitter-patter. Caleb will be the one to discover the rain is gummy bears. He and his sister will dash outside, onto the sidewalks, laughing as gummies—red, blue, green—fall from the sky, pelting their heads and arms and shoulders. They will face the sky, catching them in their mouths, grabbing from the air, slipping on sidewalks covered with them.

Bear Sightings

After dinner with friends, while her husband John disappears for a coffee in the kitchen, Chloe tells the story about the day her baby daughter faced down two bears. Years ago, when Chloe was alone with Avery in the Blue Ridge Mountains, a black bear cub poked its nose at Avery, who was lying tummy-down on a blanket in the grass. Chloe could see a full-grown bear waiting just within sight. That was why, Chloe says, her daughter Avery was never afraid—not of her parents, not of the neighborhood boys on their bikes, not of anyone. Like Davy Crockett, but a peaceful sort, she escaped unharmed. That's the way Chloe tells it, the highly curated version she shares with friends.

Chloe feels herself come alive, briefly, when she tells the story and watches the astonished faces of their guests. She can feel her own face heating up, her voice growing louder, and when she gets to the point of almost losing Avery, her eyes fill with tears. It doesn't matter that Avery, a young woman now about to leave for college, rolls her eyes at the story, or that John leaves the room when she tells it, Chloe says it really happened that way.

When John returns with the coffee, Chloe, flushed with wine and full of cheer, excuses herself to the long porch outdoors and settles onto a swing. She listens for the crickets picking up in the evening air and thinks of an old friend from work, who loved her stories. She reflects that although her own life is unremarkable, she did produce something as vibrant and fearless as Avery, which proves, after all, there was something of that liveliness within her too.

Alone now on the swing, Chloe recalls another version of the story she keeps for herself. The true story of the bears actually began on a cold evening three years into their marriage, with John standing, arms crossed, facing away, in the bedroom doorway.

The argument had started over something small, maybe the way she had left dishes in the sink, or how little they'd seen of each other's bodies since Avery came along. While Chloe spoke to John's thick, dark hair and the broad outline of his back, he spoke to the hallway in front of him. After a few minutes of that, he had left for the basement. She was still in their bedroom, the way they'd been sleeping for weeks.

John would sleep in, and she would wake up early with the baby, feeding her, changing her, and on to the second bottle of the day before John got out of bed for work. From the beginning, because she'd taken leave from work, and he hadn't, Chloe had agreed to take the nighttime and early morning wakenings. John slept so deeply, particularly in the mornings, it was almost as though he were hibernating.

The arrangement seemed to work at first, but it was the second bottle that got her. John had no idea what went on between five and eight in the morning, or between the first and second bottles. It was Chloe and Avery's dawn alone.

That night as she tossed in bed after the argument, Chloe wondered what would happen if they disappeared entirely during those early hours. She could head west from their Northern Virginia home and be into the Shenandoah Valley by the time John got up for coffee. She could have Avery in a backpack—didn't they have a hiking pack somewhere? She could be coming up over a ridge by the time he realized they weren't there. Didn't every young mother dream some version of this? Chloe suspected so, even if they later conveniently forgot.

Things were all right now when Avery was too young to notice much, but sometime in the next three or four years, she would start to see her mother rolling her eyes at John, complaining about the chores, and John telling her to fuck off. And then, later, either say he was joking or erupt into another hot fury—or she'd overhear Chloe yelling back at John, and that's what would stick in her memory. Her mother, who either yelled or took the yelling. Those were Chloe's only two choices in this marriage—predator or prey.

So, Chloe determined that in the morning when Avery woke, she would leave. It was the idea of Avery as an adult, asking her why she was that way, whichever way she would choose.

Chloe and Avery awoke at five-thirty in the morning and were on the road by six. Chloe liked driving in the dark, early spring. The worst of the morning rush wouldn't hit for another hour. Chloe was out of the city in twenty minutes and onto the long, black highway. She chose a selection of Bach—piano—to listen to. It felt like the greatest luxury in the world to listen to her own music in the quiet of the car. Was this all happiness required? A cold, quiet drive?

Wasn't this, anyway, what John got from life? A quiet, happy baby, already napping by the time he woke? The knowledge that all was taken care of, the baby in good hands, and then, with the press of a button, a hot coffee consumed in a silent house? How easy it all must seem to him.

Now, with Avery in the back, asleep again, and the music in the car at a low volume, Chloe breathed a sigh of relief. She listened to the piano rising and falling and watched the black roads around her. The edges of trees, the lit up lower halves of trunks, zipped around her on either side of the highway.

Chloe felt she was in a dream. When the road dipped down, the headlights lit up more. When it rose, as it did the farther west she drove, the headlights shone lower, and it was like the darkness descending from above.

This couldn't possibly be her life, alone, in the quiet morning. She was barely outside the city now, on the interstate, and already she felt as though she'd entered someone else's secret life. Everyone was going at a tremendous speed. Eventually, the city air would give way to hills, and the cars would grow increasingly sporadic. John would still be under the covers in the basement.

Chloe replayed their conversation from the previous night. She had been telling John that very night that her world felt small, that she was tired of their suburban life and the same mothers who shopped at the same Safeway, and that she regretted leaving her job.

And John had exploded. Hadn't she been the one to ask to leave her job? And wasn't he providing for all of them now? Well, yes, but it wouldn't be forever. Just until Avery got older.

The problem was Chloe was never sure which comment would set things off with John. He would get furious about the smallest things. A doctor who mischarged him. Little indignities of the day. Mostly, this fury was not directed at her, but the heat of it consumed the air in the house, until there wasn't anything else to breathe.

Chloe thought about John as a spigot of water, sometimes comfortably warm, but sometimes, suddenly, scalding, blistering her skin, followed by an icy cold spell for a long time afterward. Chloe couldn't stay in the bath, but couldn't quite make herself get out, either. There was always the prospect of another comfortably warm spell.

Did other couples live like this? Secret furies, nursed for hours and through the night, interspersed with brief interludes of—not happiness, maybe, but comfort? Was anyone truly happy? Chloe didn't know. Sometimes, she wished she could understand how others lived. Were her friends happy in their marriages? Was anyone? If they were, perhaps she should finally leave John. If they weren't happy, if no one was, then it made sense to carry on.

She kept driving. Along the way, it occurred to her she might find a cabin to stay in. Chloe could find more formula at a grocery store, but she'd need a fridge for other things.

She came to a gas station and filled up. Avery was sleeping in the back. Chloe hated to move her, but she didn't want to leave her in the parking lot alone, so she pulled out the carrier and kept her in it.

Inside the bright gas station, an older woman with stiff, dyed blonde hair paused at the counter and eyed Chloe and the baby.

"Doesn't she need a blanket in the cold?"

"It's all right," Chloe said, doubting herself even as she said it. "We're just here a moment."

"Poor little feet."

The woman was buying a carton of cigarettes and an orange juice. Chloe bought a coffee and some granola bars. She was keenly aware of how she must appear, dressed in jeans and a cheap cotton shirt, with a diaper bag and a baby, this time of morning, and no one waiting for her in the car.

Avery stirred awake and began to cry, confirming, Chloe was sure, the woman's suspicions that Chloe was an unfit mother. That was how the woman looked at her, vindication in her eyes, or so it seemed. And

Chloe judged the woman, silently, as one of those women with nothing better to do than to fuss over other people's babies.

Back in the car, Chloe observed with a rising disappointment the orange glow of sun on the horizon, which meant her sojourn in solitude would soon end. The sky would lighten, and she would no longer be able to travel as the invisible woman in the dark, as she preferred. And at some point, John would call.

The sunrise was an eerie, beautiful sight, though, behind her, as she drove west. In the rearview, she could make out the black outlines of trees, and behind them, a low ribbon of glowing pink sky.

Finally, as she knew it would, her phone rang. John. Chloe hesitated and then picked up.

"Where are you?" He was just waking up. He sounded sweet.

She paused. As far as he knew, she was just out for something from the store. She wanted to hold that moment for as long as possible. When she couldn't any longer, she said, "I'm just out for a drive. I need a little space."

"With Avery?"

"Yes, of course."

"Come home."

"I need a little time."

"Chloe. I'm sorry about last night."

How many times had she heard that? How many times had he snapped and then apologized, and she'd forgiven, and then he'd snapped again. Usually, he could persuade her. This time though was different. She'd put in more than an hour of driving now. He couldn't reach her in the same way. The miles had created something new in her and weakened his gravitational pull. She said, "A little more time."

Maybe all marriages were this way; maybe he wasn't bad at all. It was so much easier to get along with him from a distance. Less pull, and also less anger. Maybe distance was the solution.

A year before Avery was born, Chloe had almost had an affair with a man from her office, a former Marine who'd settled, in a lost sort of way, into a sales role, who was bored and came by her desk, often smiling wryly, using any excuse to chat. What she had liked, most of all, was the way he threw his head back when he laughed at her stories, a genuine laugh that made the lines around his blue eyes crinkle, and his voice would rise an octave, and sometimes afterward he would keep going with little chuckles, aftershocks of delight.

Chloe had never been sure what kind of storyteller she was, but with the Marine, she found herself suddenly sure she was a good one, that she was funny and lively, because he always listened and always came back for another. With the Marine, her stories all seemed to mean something deeper. It was a shame she found that version of herself only when John wasn't around. The Marine liked best her story about hiking with her family as a child, how she climbed right up to a ridge but then was too scared to cross it, how she had to scoot back down on her bottom, how frightened she was of any heights at all.

They had started having lunch every day at a café down the street from their office, he talking about television shows he liked and she talking vaguely about wanting changes in her life.

One day, next to the salad bar, he'd edged his foot right up against hers under the table. Her heart beat furiously inside her. And when she blushed and didn't move her foot, he put a hand just above her knee.

Chloe toyed with the idea of inviting the Marine out for drinks that night, daydreaming about how exactly she would cross whatever unreturnable threshold would take her toward what she knew they both wanted.

Instead, she had gone home that evening and told John that she had decided, firmly, to leave her job. She said she was tired of it, ready to stay home and try for a baby. That was her decision, and when she said she was still really sure after a few more days, he had agreed. Chloe suspected, sometimes, that was why John seemed so confused by her disappointment with their life. Because, after all, it had been her decision.

On the other end of the line, John mumbled something about needing to get ready for work and asked her to call soon. Actually, leaving had been easier than she'd feared, and now she felt a shiver of pleasure. What would she do now? Another coffee perhaps, another stop. The whole day stretched in front of her, a road to be discovered. The sun lit up around her.

At the next rest stop, where Chloe stopped for a second coffee, she saw again the same blonde, feathery hair, the woman who'd spoken with her before. They must have been on the same path. Chloe couldn't believe it. To her relief, this time, Avery was wrapped warmly in a blanket. Chloe headed to the counter with the coffee.

This time, a man was with the woman. He had gray hair and a long chin and said, "Sheila, we don't have all day."

Chloe was embarrassed for the woman, Sheila—who must've been self-conscious herself—and felt suddenly a surge of warmth toward her. She was sorry she'd thought poorly of the woman earlier. At least John would never speak that way in public.

Sheila seemed not to register the man's voice. Chloe caught the woman's eye then, and pointed to the baby's feet. She said, "See, I covered her," but the woman simply took in a deep breath and looked at her quizzically, like she didn't remember Chloe or Avery, and then after a long exhale, said, "Oh, that's nice." What Chloe couldn't get over was the woman's vacant eyes, as though she were actually far away, inhabiting another space, and all that was left was her body.

When the man became impatient and left for the car, Chloe watched the woman's shoulders drop, as if she were releasing a great tension, and then she joined Chloe at the coffee station, but neither of them spoke again.

Although Chloe didn't know the woman, she still, somehow, wanted the woman to acknowledge what a good mother she was. She wanted connection. She knew it wouldn't come from John. But from someone. She needed something more than she had at home, which was women she went out with every couple of weeks and shared funny stories with over drinks. More than discussing diaper changes and future preschools. More even than her dearest friends, who would've held her hands and let her cry if she'd wanted, not that she did want that. She wanted something more. Love, maybe. Or maybe simply, to feel seen as a whole person.

That would be Avery one day—she hoped. Chloe knew she had maybe ten or twelve years at the most of her daughter's unconditional love, before Avery too would see her flaws and want to drift away, and who could blame her? It was the same with mothers and children through all of history. And Chloe knew it wasn't fair to saddle Avery with all of that. Avery would have to go her own way, and she'd be ready to let go when the time came. But for now—just right now, she was so very glad to have Avery.

Avery began to cry now, bored, or stuck, or lonely. Chloe wished for a friend to travel with her, to sit in the back and tend to Avery, but it had been her choice, after all, to take off alone.

Back on the road with her second coffee, Chloe used her phone and navigated to Shenandoah National Park, where she passed a little booth, paid a toll, and received a map in return. There was nothing in particular about Shenandoah that drew her, except there it was on the map, west of her home, a big green swath, so close to her but as different from her life as anything she could imagine.

She drove on, wondering where to go next. She made her way to the top of a hill where there were bathrooms and a little viewing area. How easy and quick it had been to come here. That was what she marveled at most of all. That this place, this little way station, only a few hours from home, had never been so very far after all. Chloe had just never taken the opportunity. And yet, this was also her life, just as much as the quiet mornings at home with the familiar sounds of the garbage truck rumbling, and the television going in the background. This too was her life and had been all this time.

Chloe pondered this as she changed Avery in the back of the car, threw out the diaper in a trash can, and prepared a bottle of formula. Then, she peered out over the edge of a railing down a steep hillside to the green tops of trees below. In the distance, a view of the gentle, blue sloping mountains opened up, but the wind was fierce. Chloe felt the wind biting and pulled her coat around herself, wrapped the baby blanket more tightly around Avery. Maybe the woman, Sheila, was right. She had been selfish running into the gas station, thinking only of her own warmth, failing to cover Avery's feet.

Then, a fog began to drift in, and the sky grew gray and misty, looking like a cold rainforest. The more Chloe thought about it, the more convinced she was, not only that she had been selfish in forgetting Avery's blanket—she thought with remorse of the baby's bare feet sticking out—but that perhaps Chloe had some deep sort of selfishness in her. Why else would she be dragging Avery all the way into a forest, for no reason other than to see that she could? Would Avery hate her too when she grew up? Well, Chloe thought, in any case, she was already here and ought to keep going.

Chloe strapped Avery into a little carrier on her front. She was getting big for it, but once Chloe tightened the pack, that helped. Avery was flush against her, and seemed to like the closeness to her mother. Avery settled quickly, with wide-open eyes, quietly watching the world, as Chloe started forward on one of the many trailheads that began there.

John didn't understand Chloe's desire for something more than the life they had. Or, perhaps he did. Perhaps he too wanted more. Chloe realized now she had never asked him. Anyway, all she could understand were her own feelings.

Say she stayed here, close to Shenandoah. Say she found a way to rent a little place and to stay alone with Avery. Then she would still be a mother, but it would be different, with the sun on her head and leaves crunching under her feet. Perhaps she would turn into something else. Something more primal, an animal mother. Chloe wondered if she could really turn herself into someone else by changing her environment.

She continued down the path, and as she did her mind quieted. She thought less about John and her life back home and observed the world around her. The grass grew taller, swishing by her feet. She saw layers of leaves and ferns and little grasses sticking up from the muddy trail. The cold, gray sky. The way the wind quieted and grew still, the deeper she got into the tree canopy.

When she got hungry, she reached into her pockets for the granola bars she'd bought and shared a little of the soft granola with Avery. Along the entire way, Chloe and Avery encountered no one else on the trail. And then, after nearly an hour of walking, Chloe came upon a little bridge leading across a river and decided to stop a while. Her phone rang again. It was John, but the reception was poor. She took Avery from the pack and let her sit in the grass. She struggled to make out John's voice and walked a little away from Avery, while Avery nibbled on another bar. Perhaps John was fully awake now, after the coffee, perhaps he'd gone to work and started his day and was irritated she wasn't around and didn't know when she'd be back.

He seemed to ask her where she was now. It was at that moment that Chloe said in a quiet voice, "Maybe I won't come back."

John was quiet for a long moment. Then, "Chloe. What the fuck?"

Now, Chloe found herself at another precipice. This unfettered morning, all she'd been able to accomplish so far, small though it was, she had done it alone. And here, the forest had unfolded perfectly in front of her, with every kind of fern and green thing, soft leaves, tender growth, like a green blanket just for her. It gave her the feeling that nature was wise and giving, and that the morning had provided for her: the coffee, the hike, her mostly calm daughter, the foggy, quiet day.

Sometimes, in the years that followed, Chloe would wake at dawn and lie in bed and remember that just a few hours from home, there were perfect crisp mornings, carpets of leaves, a long, quiet drive to get there, and wonder if it was still there that way, or if it had been a dream after all.

And since it did seem to be a dream, and became more dreamlike over the years, she would sometimes descend into a kind of trance, zooming out of her life, as though she were watching herself from far away and could observe her own existence with detachment. *Look, the woman and man are waking up together. Their hands may touch. He may put an arm around her. They might make love, if they haven't in some time, then she will get up and put some dishes away, and they will check on Avery.* And it would happen like that.

Chloe must have stayed too long after the phone call, the peanut butter and chocolate granola bar crumbs and wrappers still scattered around them. That must've been what attracted the bear cub.

It was a small, furry black creature, the size of a puppy, hopping along toward them. With a terror that seized her stomach and set her heart racing, she saw it heading for the little grassy spot and Avery still in it.

The curious cub, poking its nose first toward a wrapper and then, finding Avery. And then, behind a tree, the larger bear.

Chloe froze. The blood rushed to her head, pounding and making her deliriously dizzy. What to do?

There had been a sign along the way. What had it said? Don't feed the bears? Don't approach bears? Well, the bear had approached her. What were the options then? Attack? That was out of the question. Flee? That might trigger a chase.

She knew she should never get between an adult and baby bear. But they were together now anyway, and it was her baby too. For a brief moment, their eyes locked, hers and the mother's—she assumed it was a mother anyway, doing the work of foraging for two—two animals locked in, both trapped and undecided.

In that moment, Chloe remembered there was another option she hadn't yet considered. Where she'd seen it, she couldn't remember. Something tickled the back of her mind. Not defend or attack, not flee. *Play dead.* She wasn't sure whether it was the right move. There was a right and wrong time to do that, and she couldn't remember which was which. But the instinct overtook her. *Play dead.* That was it. She flopped on top of Avery, caving her body over her completely, giving her just enough room to breathe, in a bubble underneath her stomach, and lay perfectly still. She took in a breath and slowly released it.

In that moment, Chloe felt the smallest shift within her. What she never expected, as she played dead, as she felt the little cub sniffing at them both, was the freedom she felt, as she lay there, unmoving for what must have been a minute but seemed an eternity. Of course she was terrified. Her heart was racing in her chest. But also, alongside the terror, there it was, a giving in. Was this what it was like? Those last moments of life? An assent, no, a willingness to enter in? All this time she'd viewed the end with terror, but really, it was simple. A letting go. An unclenching of the fist. Breathing, in, out, praying the baby's soft babbles wouldn't grow louder. It was impossible to explain, even to herself, but that was what it was.

After a few moments of sniffing, the cub, apparently bored by the large, dead human, lost interest and moved back toward its parent. Chloe was now neither attacker nor prey, just boring. Boring enough to leave alone.

In the years to follow, Chloe would devote all her attention to Avery. Avery, the strong-willed child, who after all, had once been approached by a baby bear. When others expressed disbelief at her story, Chloe would answer, "That's how it happened."

What she didn't say exactly, but what she meant, was this: A little bear had approached Avery once, and after that, Avery could never be afraid again, of anyone or anything. What the story meant was that Avery's life wouldn't look anything like Chloe's.

How close Chloe had come to another life. And how easily it had all begun, the move toward it. The drive, the coffee. Another life was just a short distance beyond a gas station with hot pots of coffee, or maybe, a hand on the leg, a squeeze of fingers in return, the unraveling of the old life, weaving into something new.

Only, Chloe could never quite cross the ridge. And what might've happened if she had? Would it have been a good life? Would the feeling of that morning drive have continued? Would she have retained the rush of escape under cover of dark, the intoxicating early morning black sky, giving cold, sweet, groggy life to her lungs? Or, would it eventually have melted into the same life as before? Loneliness, solitude, another man, another emptiness closing in around her?

It was Chloe who moved first, faster than the mother bear. She was the braver one. She had moved toward Avery, the one precious being in the world to her. She understood that fact firmly in that moment. And also that at one point in her life, undoubtedly, she too had been brave.

After that, the mother bear moved forward and scooped up the cub by the scruff of its neck, its legs dangling in the air, before loping off into the forest. Chloe, too, would take Avery home, and end her journey, which felt selfish now, and which had endangered them both.

Often, in the years after her return home, Chloe forgot things. She would be pairing socks and absently leave them on the couch to get caught up in a novel. Or, she would be calling her mother for a recipe and end up abandoning the recipe to look for socks. And although she and John returned to going on dates and to making love again, Chloe suspected he could tell that her heart wasn't in it. It became one of those things in their marriage that was too delicate for either of them to approach, and often in the quiet evenings, she wondered what the Marine was up to. But the idea of striking up a conversation with him had passed too. He was a vapor now, without any passion left, who visited her consciousness from time to time. Sometimes, she heard in her own voice that absent tone she'd heard from the woman at the gas station. *Oh, that's nice.*

After the encounter with the bears, Chloe would drive back home. John would stay home from work that day. He would give Avery the next bottle and nuzzle her head under his chin. Although in the future they would fight again, the next morning, Chloe and John would wake up together in the same bed. And yet, in the version of the story Chloe kept inside her, the one she never told, she had escaped. She didn't return to John that day, never fully, never really at all.

Ain't Gonna Stick

By the time I met him, in my thirties, my expectations were properly tempered. I knew enough not to get used to the feel of his warm arms or the sweet smell of Scotch still on his breath or the peaked ceiling with the windows underneath. When he saw the morning snow falling and said, "That shit ain't gonna stick," he didn't have to tell me. I was already pulling on the clothes we'd carelessly discarded and heading out to my car. It wasn't worth waiting or even scraping off the ice, because he was right: it was already melting.

The Inner Chamber

The night I slip inside my lover's heart, I can't escape the taste of blood, nor the smell, nor the pulsing of a beat around us—*umm-pah, umm-pah*. Past the atrium, it's an entire chamber of red walls and vaulted ceilings that stretch up forever. And the women everywhere, slender, with dark, made-up eyes, amble up to bars, lounge on oversized couches, give bored smiles. He certainly has a type.

Really, I don't belong here in this club. But somehow I am past the roped-off entrance; someone has made a mistake, and I'm here.

In the real world, I am asleep, or he is, rather, on a large and gaudy four-poster bed, next to a phone that is always dinging and lighting up the room at odd hours, beside a lighter and a pack of cigarettes that go everywhere with the phone. But here, inside this heart, are high walls, and women everywhere, a long bar, and a seemingly eternal wait for a drink. I'm waiting to order a gin and tonic.

Out in the real world, it is Valentine's Day. This evening, we walked together along the pathway around the pond by his house, and he took my hand and interlaced his fingers with mine. And when the wind blew hard, I tucked my hand inside his jacket pocket. I was enchanted by the little pond and the arch at the top of a nearby bridge. But inside the jacket pocket, next to my fingers, his phone buzzed and buzzed.

I recognize a few of the women from photos, these women who take up space in my lover's heart. The woman he dated just before me leans against the back of a chair. A stream of sunlight coming from a crevice in a high wall highlights a stripe of light down one contoured cheek. She rests easily, while I crack my wrists and search for a familiar face.

I belong in a dark bar with black walls and graffiti, with dogs padding around, with a breeze, with women who take their shoes off and splay their unpainted toes. But I chose to enter this place—pretended that I was the kind of woman who enjoys staying out too late dancing after too many shots, even when I would prefer to be at home in pajamas.

A couch beside me is sticky with the residue of something that smells like bourbon, and like the others, it's already occupied. I contemplate what might happen if I leave this place. I suspect my own heart would break. Not in a metaphorical way. I mean structurally. Walls coming down, blood rushing to the center. A physical rupture.

Sometimes I envy my lover, who once told me that love doesn't disappear, it simply moves on. Is this what he meant? Is love a ballroom, bouncing from one person to another? To have a heart as big as a ballroom would be easier. I can barely fit anyone into mine. My friends say I will make room for others after him, but I'm not sure. The walls of my heart are already taut, stretched like the skin of a pregnant belly, near rupture with memories.

There is something off about the women inside this chamber. His high school sweetheart has a graceful, fawn-like face. But the real one, from photos I've seen at his mother's, had a more confident look, less afraid, sturdier and with fuller cheeks.

And here is the woman he was still with in our earliest days together. "We weren't quite exclusive yet," he told me. "I wish you could get inside my heart and see how I feel about you." Of course, like any heart, his has cracks. They aren't so difficult to find. So, while he was sleeping, I pried one open with my fingers, so gently he couldn't feel it—and made my way inside.

"How did you meet?" I ask a woman with pink lips in a blue bridesmaid dress, lounging on a nearby couch.

"Our friends' wedding. He told me my dress was beautiful. He loved the way it lay on my body. He said the blue brought out my eyes. It was my color."

"Oh." He once told me something similar. But my dress was yellow. He said yellow was my color. He liked it on me. Now, I see it in the memories of the other women. I see them tumbling into bed. I hear him whisper, "Darling," never caring it was too soon for such intimacies.

I can hear the women's memories buzzing and pulsing around me.

"Red is your color."

"Black is your color."

"This is your color."

"Your dress."

"The way it fits over your hips."

I want out of this place. I touch my throat and feel a silver necklace. I look down and catch a flash of yellow. I am wearing a yellow cotton sundress, but my yellow dress wasn't a sundress, nor was it quite so bright. I wore the yellow dress the warm afternoon in early fall when I met him for coffee and he was pulsing with energy and talking too quickly. When he stared into my eyes across the table and I surprised him with a kiss.

Once, during a rough patch, he disappeared for most of a night and wouldn't say where he went. I pressed, and finally he said he'd walked all the way around the pond by his house, paced alongside the geese, and tried to think through what to do about us.

"What did the geese advise?" I'd asked. But he didn't crack a smile and didn't answer either. I could see then he wasn't thinking of the bridge, or the geese, or about us at all.

I touch my lips, and a trace of red comes off on my finger. I don't wear lipstick. But the woman I am here wears sundresses and bright red lipstick. My hair is thicker and straighter, the way he always wanted me to wear it, my weight sits differently on my body. And it's early fall, the way it was when we met, and then it hits me.

I exist here only as a specific version of myself—his version. I can feel how he wanted me, and not just that, a deeper feeling. Love, eventually. And I see it will end.

This woman in the yellow dress, who is me, will end it. Because she has seen inside him, and at the end of it, she couldn't find an empty couch or a chair in this place and didn't want to compete for a place to sit.

And I feel, with certainty—his certainty—that there will be others after me. It is not a profound or enlightening moment. I am just tired. I want to wipe off the lipstick and take off the yellow dress and put on sweatpants, but I can't, because he doesn't remember me like that, and I'm trapped. This has always been my problem. I've rarely had a good exit strategy, can't think of one even now.

With each deafening beat, the walls of his heart grow outward, ever expanding, and mine shift ever so slightly too. My own heart is a delicate structure, made by a shoddy engineer. Poorly framed, thin materials, cracks everywhere. I feel the walls starting to crumble. It won't be long now. And with the collapse will come my own exit.

I see now how it will end, the very night. He will cook dinner. He'll text another woman. He'll ask me a dozen times how I am feeling. He will kiss my forehead and step out for a cigarette with his phone.

In the morning, his arms will wrap around me even as his eyes drift somewhere else. In his heart, that expansive chamber, the walls will continue to balloon outward. With each beat, I see his walls growing wider, the ceiling higher, the space emptier even as more women enter it—at least as many more after me as came before me. The women are bored and lonely, and he has given them nothing to quench hunger or thirst.

I can't help but notice how the other women, as I once did, seem to confuse his intent gaze, the upward curve of his mouth, with something weightier. How refined they seem, how lovely, how practiced in saying the right things. But they are not stupid: they don't believe they are the only ones. They, too, know that they have many other colors beyond those they wear here. The ballroom will never feel sufficiently full—his own brand of horror. If I had to guess, I would say he is sorry for the way he is.

I am sorry, too, for making believe that I was another kind of woman. There was a certain satisfaction in occupying this chamber, this space, where we appeared to be brighter and more vibrant than any place outside. It was nice, for a little while, to pretend.

Brown-Eyed Recluse

Nine months after Isabelle's husband left, Isabelle lay on her rumpled bedspread, feeling a rattling in her stomach, like a marble rolling inside her. She drew a hand across her belly, protectively. She counted the rumbling as a sign her appetite was finally returning, and tried to think of what might satisfy the feeling, some toast and jam perhaps.

In the first days after the split, Isabelle's therapist had warned her about surfacing her feelings too quickly. She'd promised her that with time, Isabelle's appetite would return. So, Isabelle distracted herself. She went outside to sit in a nearby park. She watched ants marching, bees looping around flowered bushes, a spider dangling from a wooden beam, and remembered that as a child, she'd thought she might become a biologist. But now she was taking a break from her temp job and trying to understand the numb emptiness inside her. After the park, she would have a bite for dinner and then sleep. Isabelle's favorite time, day or night, was some ten minutes after taking a small cylindrical white pill, sometimes two. Then she would read until her body could no longer resist, until her head and heart and limbs screamed for sleep, right up to the last possible moment she could bear it. And only then would she tumble into an instant slumber.

When the toast with jam and coffee failed to satisfy, Isabelle rummaged in the kitchen for something else. She whispered to herself, "What is it then, inside me," and then, "Come out, you little thing." And then, perhaps a hallucination, a remnant of the pill from the night before, she felt a stirring inside her, like a baby might turn in the womb.

Then, the rattling welled up, like a sob or laugh. As she willed it forward, the way a mother must feel when she goes into labor, Isabelle began to shake from the inside. Something moved upward from inside her, and she saw in a bedroom mirror one brown and spindly leg protruding from her mouth, then two. She sprinted to the bathroom and heaved. Out onto the tile floor tumbled an eight-legged creature, brown, smooth, and delicate, a spider the size of a lime and covered in mucus like a newborn baby. The gnawing emptiness that had been inside her was now gone.

On fresh and nervous legs, the spider crawled to her bedroom, past the little corner where Isabelle had imagined a crib might go someday, leaving a trail of mucus behind it. As Isabelle peeked in from the hallway, she saw it devour three dried out succulents from the windowsill, a taped-up box of photo albums, and a bookshelf. Growing at a tremendous rate, it devoured a dresser and a mirror. Then it stretched its mouth over one corner of the bed, the way a snake's mouth engulfs a rodent, and soon had grown large enough to swallow the bed completely. Isabelle sighed with relief when her belongings disappeared (they reminded her of *him*, after all) and more than that, the spider was not after her. In fact, she swore she could feel its thoughts. It was not malicious—just hungry.

Still, it was better to be out of the way. Isabelle went down the stairs and left her apartment building in the tights, sweatshirt, and slippers she had been wearing for more than a week.

The spider climbed out the window and spun a thread to lower itself to the sidewalk. Once there, it devoured the entire apartment building, leaving a scar on the sidewalk a half-block long. Only the concrete foundation remained where the building had been. Although Isabelle knew she should mourn the people who'd been inside, she felt only the familiar empty numbness.

"Where does the emptiness come from?" Isabelle had asked her therapist months before. Her therapist had smiled nervously and said, "Goodness, my degree is in social work, not philosophy."

The spider lifted its delicate brown legs in a trot and headed for the neighborhood pool beside Isabelle's former building, pressed its mouth to the water, and slurped. Isabelle remembered spending the summer lying in bed, staring at the sunlight sneaking onto her bedsheets in light fingers, summer and swimming going on without her.

Isabelle turned then to the spider and asked, "Aren't you going to swallow me too?"

By now, the spider had grown so large she couldn't see its full body unless it bent down, so she was really speaking to one joint of a skinny leg. She longed for the thing to open its mouth and take her inside. She wanted to experience the nothingness of its belly, to occupy it as it had occupied her.

The spider knelt down and peered at her with its eight shiny eyes. Isabelle grew hopeful. But when the eyes locked with hers, Isabelle noticed a resemblance to her own brown irises. This was a creature knitted in the deepest recesses of her lonely heart. She was its mother, and it did not want to eat her. That's what the look meant.

The spider straightened up and moved on without Isabelle. As she watched, it devoured the whole neighborhood, then the city. Office buildings crumbled, the skyline shifted, the shadows of the city cleared, and Isabelle saw the whole sky and hills in the distance. She watched the spider's silhouette tearing and feasting on the hills, leaving a flat, scarred landscape everywhere and a whipping wind with nothing but Isabelle to catch on.

The spider went on to eat the sun and moon, planets, and entire constellations. Then it settled into an empty blackness and began to gnaw on the first joint of its own leg, like a dog. It bit off the lower half, then consumed it. The hungry spider went on, gnashing more and more wildly, swallowing chunks of its own head, devouring its own eyes like grapes, saving the final two legs for the very end, until all that was left was a black hole, unrecognizable except for two venomous fangs. And only then, after Isabelle whispered, "Please," did the spider finally allow her to draw near enough to feel the gravitational pull of its open maw and the most exquisite, lulling feeling of surrender, like the very last moment before slumber.

The Long Brew

8 a.m.

The baby wakes and mews, soft and persistent as a kitten. You rise from bed, lift her from a bassinet as you catch her floppy head in your palm, and nurse her. She is still uncoordinated, hands fluttering, mouth sputtering, not yet smiling. She's fresh and new, like a warm thing pulled from the dirt. You're exhausted. When she falls asleep at your breast, you set her down and fill the coffee filter with grounds. Before you finish, she's up again.

10 a.m.

You did not add the water, a simple oversight from lack of sleep. You smell the pot burning dry in the kitchen. The baby eats and poops while you wait to fall in love with her. Her eyes fix on you, and you gaze back, then down to your phone, and over to the kitchen where the pot is making steaming sounds but no drips, and back again. Her eyes are gray, like the winter sky outside. You add water to the pot and long for the first bitter sip.

Noon

When your mother calls, you can't account for the time. Surely you weren't feeding and changing her the entire morning, but you can't say exactly what happened, only that you've barely eaten or slept. You tell her you've noticed new lines around your eyes in the mirror and joke that the baby is already stretching out of her clothes. She tells you babies have a way of pocketing time, maybe in the folds of their tiny skin, or their clothes. Who can say? When your mother swears that only this morning you were a newborn, you roll your eyes. Only when you hang up do you realize you haven't poured the coffee yet, and already it smells old, like the inside of a gas station.

2 p.m.

You finally take the first sip. It's burned, but good enough. You notice a hunch in your back. When you stretch your arms to the ceiling, something catches and makes you wince. You sip and wonder where she'll go to school. The steam swirls up in the cup. You promise yourself you'll have another sip. But she needs you first.

4 p.m.

You nod off on the couch. You dream you are on a train, rolling past a brown and white winter landscape. Trees with sleeping, bare branches slip by. You wrap your hands around a warm cup of black coffee. The smell, it seems, has worked its way into your dreams. You awaken, unable to sleep in long stretches anymore. You hear crying, you think, but it's a hallucination. Then you realize it's been quite some time since she's cried. You check on her, and she is fine. You tuck a blanket around her. She looks up, barely registers you, and settles back to sleep.

6 p.m.

The lukewarm black cup goes down in gulps. You remember long ago when you worked in a coffee shop, sipping all day at leisure, before kids. When you made out with the other barista in the back, laughed at the coffee stains on his apron, and swore you would never turn out like the suburban women who came in with baby strollers for nonfat lattes. You could swear she's grown even in the last hours. There is a wise look to her now. You finish the cup and pour another. It's too late for this much caffeine, but you've waited and waited for it, and the night will be long.

8 p.m.

You doze briefly and wake again. She seems to need you less. The desperate mews, the quivering, are all long gone. Your fingertips are jittery, but there's some coffee left, so you pour another cup. What else is there to do? You ponder the empty minutes in front of you. The house is so quiet, you can hear each tick of the clock. You grab a book, but your eyes struggle to focus. Suddenly, you need glasses. You stare at yourself in the mirror and swear you didn't have any gray the last time you checked. And the baby you picked up this morning? That bleating being with crust in her eyes and milk at the corners of her mouth? She's reaching for the door. Before you finish the cup, she'll be gone.

In the Great Grown-Up Game of Make-Believe

Erin plays the part of the heroine. Cast for her soft lips and full body, she throws herself into relationships with gusto. She has mastered the laugh where she pulls back her lips, bares her teeth, and squints like she's sharing an intimate joke. Roland, cast opposite her, is chosen for his bravado. He's been practicing for this role his whole life, since plastic sword fights with his brothers, who rolled him onto his back and pinned his shoulders to the ground, tip of the sword on the Adam's apple.

In the opening scene, Erin enters Roland's apartment carrying an overnight bag disguised as a purse. Roland puts a comedy routine on the TV. He watches out of the sides of his eyes for a laugh to rise up from Erin's chest. Head tosses backward. Shoulders shake.

Just before a punchline, Erin rests her fingertips on Roland's back, feels the tautness of his muscles, and when the moment comes, releases a giggle that sends her whole body rocking backward onto a cushion. She isn't sure whether it's the three glasses of wine she's had, or the feeling of delight in her chest—Roland's hand on her knee, a gentle squeeze.

Erin has always been attuned to tight muscles, micro movements, quick shifts in mood, like the tensing of her father's jaw or the clenching of a fist. She has perfected the art of a disarming smile. Erin has been on the lookout for love since she left home at seventeen. She has been practicing for this role since she was a girl and discovered the difference between dialogue—*I love you*—and stage action—a door kicked open, doorknob punching a wall.

On their first date, Erin caught the gleam of desire in Roland's eyes, opened her purse, and found a mint. On every date since then, Roland has been waiting for a repeat of what followed: a grip on the back of his head, lips pressed against his.

At the sound of Erin's laugh, Roland turns onto his back and exposes the soft front of his neck. Erin remembers something her parents once said about becoming one of *those women*—wasting time with *those men*, interested in one thing only. Erin isn't sure how to trust her judgment, but she knows she's remarkable at assuming a role. The scene is set, and Erin will stay over and return home in the early morning.

Erin is a little sorry for the look of hope, and maybe affection, on Roland's slender face, and she'll be sorry months later, after she breaks it off, when he calls to ask after her dogs, when he texts her over the new year, and later on her birthday, but not sorry enough to break character, which would make her feel silly and small for having to explain her own lack of certainty over whether and when she was performing. She asks for another glass of wine, is relieved at his relief. Body arcing toward his.

Erin has tried to reimagine herself into a thousand different roles, successful like her brother, outgoing and beloved like her sisters, but each time, her imagination falls short, and as she sees the look of desire on Roland's face, she knows she is good at least at this one thing, which has proven results again and again, perhaps the thing she is best at, perhaps the only thing. And though she knows this power she has is fleeting, she has it now, and she cannot bear to disappoint her audience. Erin is a little sorry for the way she is. She has, she fears, mastered the art of performance to such a degree that she prefers it to the alternative. The alternative being that all the world's a stage, but she's not on it and thus, ceases to exist. The alternative being that if no one is watching her, Erin will quietly disappear.

Roland is contemplating what the kind of man Erin could love would do next. These days, he barely speaks to his brothers and wouldn't know what sort of advice to ask if he did. Days ago, he bought an extra bottle of wine to keep in case Erin asked, and wrote a note confessing how often he thinks of her. He imagines an entire life with her, buying those little boxes of mints for her at the grocery store. He replays in his mind the giggle that makes her sound like a girl when she tucks her arm into his side. He imagines how her expression will look when she unfolds the small note he scrawled in pen, when her eyes rest upon the words, *falling for you*. Then he'll remember his brothers, their plastic swords tipping toward him, how small he felt—the role he can't seem to break free of. He gets up for the extra bottle. At the last minute, he'll conceal the note in the trash can underneath a couple of paper napkins and a wine cork. Fold, tuck.

It Wasn't a Fit

Fit: Suitability

Since her divorce two years ago, Emma has dated several different men. One went on about the quality of the local schools during long brunches that dragged into the afternoons. One cooked elaborate dinners with her on Friday nights and left early on Saturdays to run. She thinks most of all about another who stopped responding to her texts and wonders whether he was the one.

Fit: To make a place or room for

Emma's apartment is on the top floor of what used to be a house, in a neighborhood of red brick homes, each like the other, that face a courtyard of historic trees—historic means don't touch. One of the trees stretches up over the other trees like it's trying to get the last fresh breath of air.

Fit: To be in harmony with

Emma's parents, who have been together for more than three decades, are renovating their house. They ask which kind of tile she thinks might suit their kitchen. Emma says they're the ones who ought to know.

Fit: Able to meet the required purpose

Some evenings after the kids go down, Emma pours red wine for herself into a sippy cup because she can't find a proper glass.

Fit: To be seemly or proper

The other neighborhood women, outside on their porches with their husbands and kids and dogs, have a *look* when Emma approaches.

Fit: The degree of closeness between surfaces in an assembly of parts

Emma gives her children a puzzle to put together, but they sob because the last piece is missing. They scream so loud that Emma's ears ring. Emma leaves the room, flops onto her bed, and stares up at the ceiling. She wants to know what to do now with all the other pieces.

Fit: To conform correctly

When Emma fought with her sisters as a child, her father would send them to their separate rooms to think it over, but when the doors closed, Emma never thought it over. Instead, she imagined she had been dropped into the wrong family.

Fit: In good shape

Emma thinks that maybe the answer she's looking for has something to do with the feeling in her chest when she goes on a long run by herself, feels the cool air cycling through her lungs, and imagines that with each run, her body is changing ever so slightly.

Fit: A sudden burst of activity

Emma transfers her children out of one elementary school and into another.

Fit: An impulsive or irregular manner

Emma runs into a neighbor who is with the homeowners association, who tells Emma the trees in the courtyard are heritage trees, which means they're large and irreplaceable. She says their roots are connected and that each tree can feel the trauma or loss of any other. She says that's why Emma's kids shouldn't be swinging on the branches. Emma pretends to contemplate the sky overhead.

Fit: An emotional reaction, as of anger or frustration

Emma asks a friend one day, "You know that feeling where you try and try and try to find the answer for how to live your life, but the definition is always shifting, and then you start to wonder if maybe you're the one who isn't right?"

Antonyms: Unsuitable, improper, inappropriate, unbecoming, unhappy, unseemly, wrong

Emma puzzles over the last words her husband said to her before they split, about their not being a fit, and in what ways they, or anything at all, are meant to fit. She puzzles so long that the words themselves lose meaning. The individual pieces of her life seem fine enough, but Emma can't figure out how to assemble them anymore. Emma thought autumn was her favorite season, but with the darkening of the skies in the late afternoons, and the end of the warm season pressing upon her, she wonders if it wasn't spring. It's becoming more difficult to decide. She struggles with a snug running shoe and wishes she could find someone who can tell her whether there truly are different seasons of life and whether another season is coming.

Evening by the Lake

When my little sister, Ruby, won't stop screaming, Mom grabs her around the waist, hoists her up on one hip, and tells Dad, "I'm taking her for a walk." Ruby is screaming because she wants to go swimming, but it's December. She's nearly four years old now and ought to know better. Dad will work on fixing the bed while they're out. He has a wooden plank on the kitchen table, hooked up to a metal clamp to hold it steady while he drills a hole. This is supposed to replace the boards that split when Ruby jumped on her bed and broke through, sending the mattress sagging to the floor.

Ruby is more trouble than I ever was, but she and Mom are the true bond of the family, Mom and Ruby going on errands together, Ruby practically glued to Mom's hip at every moment. But this time, I grab Mom's hand and insist I'm coming along too, and it's only after Dad sides with me that Mom relents.

Mom and I hold hands, even though I'm twelve now and too old for it, with Ruby—too old for this too—wailing on Mom's hip. We leave our townhome, all the way out to the Oldsmobile parked a block away, while the cars on the nearby highway whoosh by. People rush around us, clutching their long coats in the wind, waiting at crossing lights in the dark between the trucks and big rigs. The sun is just down, and the winter sky is darkening. In the older parts of Alexandria, the streets are cobblestone and the lights are strung for Christmas, but this is a newer and, I already know, poorer part of the city. It's not dangerous, just ugly. Dad moved here first, after he lost his job years ago, when he stopped talking to anyone at all, even to Mom and me, for two whole years.

Highways crisscross everywhere. On either side of one highway, which we can see from our townhome, are tall apartment complexes, lit with windows of light, many ringed with tiny blinking Christmas lights. We pass them as we leave our neighborhood and join the cars on the main roads around us.

As the highway rumbles beneath us, we pass rows of warehouses and a bus depot, which give way to the emptiness of the night, green highway signs flashing, an old amusement park where my parents met as children, now shuttered. Ruby has quieted now and is staring through the black windows.

In the decades to come, the amusement park will finally come down to accommodate more highway, but this is the early nineties, seared into my memory as a series of long drives with my mother, with few questions and little to break up the monotony. A theme park, a golf course, all to be replaced, memories that aren't mine already on their way out before my arrival. An entire city of deconstruction. These years are filled with highways and my mother's bangs waving in the wind when she rolls the window down a crack—round and round with the knob—and remembers something inaccessible to me. And large plastic glasses, and her talking quietly sometimes to herself. And Ruby and me, sitting in the back of the Oldsmobile, which is holding barely above whatever temperature it is outside.

We drive down the long highway, for thirty minutes and more, so long I decide Mom would've told Dad we were driving this far if she'd wanted him to know, but since she didn't say, it must be a secret. "Where are we going?" Ruby finally asks, and I know enough to know to say, "Quiet, Ruby. We're just driving to calm you down."

Except a little after that, we do stop, in a long, dark parking lot that gives me a funny feeling in my stomach, and then Mom takes us both by the hands, and we get out and start walking. All the way across the parking lot, to a sidewalk, and then I see around us a townhome community like ours, except quieter, darker, and lonelier. There is a little mailbox and tangle of homes and sidewalks, and then on the other side, a black lake.

Ruby squeals as we approach the lake. Somehow, she already seems to know where we're headed. There are geese pecking at the edges of the water. The great adventure, the entire point of this trek, for Ruby, is satisfied in the black-and-white creatures. Then I see Mom watching me, and I don't see why I'm the one she's watching when Ruby is the one flapping her hands and squealing, and getting way too close to the geese, who are not one bit afraid of us.

I follow Mom's eyes then to a little bridge over part of the pond, and a clearing where a man and boy are walking together, and an image rushes into my mind. The geese, some bread crusts, a hand reaching down, another man whose face escapes me.

I say, "Have we been here before?" But Mom doesn't answer.

Ruby does, though. She says, "Mommy and I feed the geese here." I never knew that. And it strikes me that I've begun already my departure into adulthood, while Ruby alone occupies a special place as Mom's baby.

And then in a moment, another person approaches, a blonde, heavy woman in a long-sleeved plaid shirt under an open coat, who stretches her arms out to my mother, calling her *Ellie*, though everyone else calls my mother by her proper name, Helen.

She smiles down at Ruby and then turns sharply to my mother and points at me and gasps. "Oh my Lord, if it isn't Jane it's her identical twin!" And now I'm baffled, staring between my mother and the woman, who seemed to be expecting us.

"Well, Jane," she says, looking to me, no introduction, "Do you want some birdseed for the geese? But come in first." She calls the last part over her shoulder as we're already following her along a sidewalk and up a set of concrete stairs, away from the lake. Mom has to drag Ruby, who is interested only in the geese.

When I see the steps going up, and the little row house, I exclaim, "Oh!" Because I recognize the row house, except it's different now. The American flag outside is gone. And now I remember the face I was trying to place earlier on the lake. Merry blue eyes with creases around their edges. Red hair. A man. Another home. This one. A place we lived years ago, maybe the first place I remember at all.

When we enter the home and the light flips on, I see the woman has the same blue eyes as the man Mom and I lived with for two years before Ruby was born—a memory so vague I sometimes question whether it really happened. But inside, it rushes back to me. The striped rug, the voluminous brown couch. *Pepper*. I hear the jingles of his collar, and Pepper runs to me, diving into me so hard he knocks me into the couch, paws on me, whining with joy, tail wagging so hard I think it's going to come off and take flight. Pepper is pawing me into the folds of the couch, Ruby is laughing, and the blonde woman is alternately yelling at the dog and saying, "Oh Gawd, Ellie, I'm going to cry."

Then she turns to me and says, "How old are you now, Jane? Thirteen? Fourteen?"

"Twelve," my mother says. "But she's an old soul." Mom says that about me, but the odd thing is, so do the teachers at school. I imagine a tattered soul stirring within me, frayed at the edges, worn down already. I don't like the term. But I do like being mistaken for fourteen.

"I know you must remember Pepper, Jane. Do you remember me too?" And when I shake my head, she says, "I was Justin's sister. Am. Well." She turns to my mother. "She remembers?"

"You remember Justin?" my mother asks. The name gives me a shock, the way it always does. It's a word my mother speaks only when we're alone, only on one of her long drives, and Dad is far away, and my mother mumbles to herself under her breath, holding conversations with someone who isn't Ruby or me. My mother's tone is plaintive, almost desperate for me to say yes.

The memories are vague. I used to ask Mom to show me pictures of him, which she keeps in an envelope in her bedroom closet under her shoes, and I'm not sure whether it's the pictures or the man I remember.

But when I hear the question—do I remember?—I walk without answering to the Christmas tree in the corner, to an ornament from Shenandoah, where we hiked together that last year. I come right up to it and trace my fingers along the black bear's face, above the lettering, *Have a Beary Merry Christmas.* And Mom and the woman exchange a look, because they know I do remember something, and my mother's face is suffused with relief.

It was Christmastime like now when we hung that ornament. There was a tree in the window like this one. We opened the door to a pack of carolers. Mom and Justin were fighting, as they sometimes did, but they had to pause long enough for the carolers to get through their set, and I stood behind them and watched, grateful for their voices. And when they'd gone, the magic held, the fight was over, and Justin had opened his arms, and how quickly Mom had gone into them.

Afterward, Justin opened a box of chocolates, which we shared, and Mom got angry at us for leaving the wrappers all over the couch. And we watched Christmas movies, like Mom's favorite, *Meet Me in St. Louis*, and sang along. I jumped on the coffee table, where I was never allowed to stand at any other time, and the whole living room was bright and merry. Then I felt guilty that I loved Justin so much that I'd forgotten about my own very serious father, celebrating Christmas alone somewhere far away in Alexandria, and guilty that in my secret heart, I'd wished Justin were my father instead.

Dad, my sweet dad, so hardworking and solemn, but with such strict rules and an unbending sense of order brought from the countryside where he grew up. Justin was fun-loving and told terrible jokes, and now I think of him, that face, that irrepressible smile, and him, cold and buried in the ground, and I can't bear it.

"Are you already set for Christmas?" the woman asks my mother, and she nods. "And Alan?" as if by afterthought. My father.

"He's well," my mother says, sounding clipped.

The woman nods and disappears into the kitchen, while Ruby is wrapping her little arms around the dog, chanting *Peppa, Peppa*. The woman returns after a moment with two small bags of birdseed for Ruby and me and a mug of hot spiced tea for my mother.

"Would you two like to go feed the geese?" the woman asks me. Ruby, torn between the dog in front of her and the idea of geese, decides not, and I shake my head too. I don't believe the woman has any children, or she'd know it's not safe to send Ruby and me out to the water in the black of night, and with Ruby so young. And I'm shocked my mother doesn't tell her so, but sits there waiting to see what I'll say. Instead, I decide to remind her I'm not a little girl like Ruby. I say, "No thank you. May I have a tea as well?" And the woman says of course and disappears to the kitchen again to grab another.

And then Mom and the woman start talking about the house. The woman says there's no sense trying to sell what won't sell right now, the market being what it is. That she sold her condo instead, which was smaller. Then there's more about paying off the house, and debt from the estate, and what she calls Justin's *extravagance*.

While they're going on about money, I start to look through the old wooden cabinet that holds up the television, and all at once, there it is, the thing I'm looking for, a long rectangle, not gone at all, the Nintendo. And so I put in a soccer game, which I'd never actually played by myself. But now I put it on, and before long, Ruby's watching, and then Mom and the other woman stop talking, and I get a goal, and then another, and I scream out. I think Mom's going to yell at me to hush, but the woman starts laughing and says, "It's so familiar, oh-my-gawd, I remember this game," and Mom says she does too.

And then the strangest thing: they join me, they actually sit down, and it's the three of us with Ruby watching from behind, and then we switch to *Duck Hunt*, and they watch me at that, and since I'm older I don't press the gun right up to the screen like Ruby does. And I have the hot tea, and I never have Mom's attention like this, never at home, where she's washing dishes or cleaning up, or getting on me about chores, but here she's completely mine, and when I hit the ducks, she and the woman cheer. And I think it's because I remind them of Justin.

"Now think about me," the woman is telling Mom, "Alone in this big house." She shrugs her big shoulders. "But I'm here. We're here. I mean. Sleeping alone is pretty good too. A big house, and only part of it still to pay off. And I have friends over. Then it feels full enough. Wait."

The woman opens up a jar on the table and hands out mint chocolates to Ruby and me. Ruby spits hers back into the wrapper because she's too little to enjoy mint, but I love mine. And then she turns on Christmas music, we wiggle our shoulders, and Mom scoops Ruby into the air. And even though I'm twelve and far too old for it, the woman lifts me up too, as I protest, and she tosses me onto the fluffy brown couch. And I yelp with the shock of it, and she says, "Oh Jane, you probably don't remember I used to scoop you up just like that when I'd come out to see you," and it's true, I don't remember her at all, just Mom and Justin.

I think of Justin with the Nintendo, screaming in joy when he'd get a goal, with a big plate of nachos he'd share with us, and a beer, a lot of beers, always jovial, always calling out and yelling, then disappearing for a smoke and returning again, ordering Taco Bell and spreading the wrappers around, not caring that it gave him, or us, indigestion, full of fun, and that word, *extravagance*. And then I start to have an idea about why I miss him so badly, and also maybe why he died.

Which, I gather, is why Mom and Dad got back together after the two-year separation. And why, although nearly every other child of divorced or separated parents dreams of their reuniting, I came home, sat quietly in my room, and missed Justin.

Justin, a name Mom would never speak again except in the privacy of the car, a memory that receded so far to the background of our lives that I started to doubt all of it ever happened. Ruby, of course, isn't in these memories because she wasn't born yet. I must've been five to seven then, and I'm twelve now and haven't been back since.

In the end, we forget the birdseed, the entire reason, I suppose, for coming into the house. Mom and the woman hug hard before we leave. It strikes me that they must love each other very much but don't see each other often, by how hard Mom is squeezing her shoulders and how the woman seems to be holding back tears.

And I wonder—at that moment—and for some reason, it's never occurred to me before, what would've happened if Justin hadn't died. If Pepper hadn't found him first, lying face down one morning on the big brown couch when I was already at school. I think Justin's death was both the worst and best thing to happen, because it brought my parents back together and made Dad get his life back together and start talking to us again, because Mom was willing to give Dad another chance.

I have the feeling now—and it feels like a big weight on my body—that I will probably be the last person alive to remember those years with Justin and Mom and me. Justin is gone now, and Mom, more likely than not, will die long before me. Ruby is no help. She wasn't even there. So that leaves just me alone to carry on to think about all that happened in those years. The Christmas tree, the carolers, the yelling for goals, and all the Taco Bell and ice cream in the world.

The woman stuffs my pockets with a variety of chocolates for the ride home, and Mom doesn't object. Afterward, on the drive back, we stop for gas and a car wash, and Mom goes on to Ruby about the car wash taking so very long that it will probably make us late. And then she goes on to say, "Isn't it nice how we fed the geese?" And there are plenty of geese closer to home, and I can see what Mom's doing with Ruby, prepping her with lines. I don't think Dad would object to Mom seeing her friend, but she doesn't want to bring it up all the same.

Ruby's no longer talking about wanting to swim, but she's begging for a dog now, and I know enough to whisper to her, "Ruby, just stop talking about dogs, and I'll sneak you some of my chocolate."

If it's possible, the drive back home is even darker. Although the clock says just after eight in the evening, it seems impossibly late. And my mother is lost somewhere, not here, in the car with us, her mind somewhere far away, as it sometimes is, so she is inaccessible to us.

I know that when we return to Dad, he will probably have fixed the planks. Ruby's bed will be back together, and I know this version of life doesn't do for Mom what the other one did, but also that it is a good enough version and that she and Dad will never leave each other again.

Ruby will not turn out like me, because she's so little and doesn't understand there's another life we might've had but didn't. She is young and simple. No one calls her an *old soul*. Dad, too, will be none the wiser. But here Mom and I are together, just the two of us, stuck in the in-between. As Ruby gnaws on a chocolate I have slipped her in the back seat, I feel the secret that binds Mom and me and surrounds us, making the two of us feel alone, and then not so alone, seeming one way and then another, like the tiny strings of lights I see in the distance, blinking on and off again—light followed by darkness followed by light.

Is She a Witch? A Quiz

1. Does she live alone, across the hallway from you, and does your daughter call her a witch? Does your daughter say any of the following while giggling, and—after you scold her—in whispers, to her friends?

   a. I hope we see the witch today.
   b. I dare you to knock on her door.
   c. Do you think she would teach us magic?

2. Is her hair carelessly styled, is she well past middle age, and has she neither disguised these facts nor disappeared from sight? Has she engaged in any of the following?

   a. Disappearing from the courtyard occupied by women in lipstick, gathering to chat in the mornings
   b. Ducking past you sometimes, as though she were hiding something
   c. Moving in a way that indicates she might occasionally like to disappear

3. Can the tinkling of a piano sometimes be heard from her apartment late at night? And if so, which of these might you identify?

   a. Beethoven
   b. Handel
   c. A classical melody of unknown origin
   d. A haunting tune that occasionally leaves you melancholy

4. Has a certain gentleman been seen to visit her apartment, with

white hair and a low voice, who could be a warlock? Does he occasionally bring any of the following with him?

a. Flowers
b. An unidentifiable herb mixed into a bouquet
c. A bottle that could contain an elixir

5. Do entire days, even weeks, pass, and you see little of her, and yet the light inside the apartment flicks on and off? Could it be—

a. She is on a retreat for witches?
b. She is using a dark and light spell?
c. She possesses the power of invisibility?

6. Does she ever give you a curious smile when you pass in the hallway? And aren't *you*, as well, a woman living without another adult at home?

a. Are you sometimes lonely?
b. Or, is it possible that feeling is an internalized norm, suggesting there is one way only to live a life?
c. As a woman?
d. At your age?
e. Meaning, with a spouse?
f. And presenting as a certain *person* in public?
g. Who never makes others uncomfortable?
h. And if you don't present in that way, you are aware, aren't you, that certain accusations may be made?

7. Have you ever felt fatigued when passing by her closed door? Such as might take place if someone were placing a hex on you?

a. Or, are you exhausted sometimes from the burdens of parenting?
b. Are you familiar with paradoxes?
c. Such as the possibility that solitude can be difficult, even as you draw toward it?

8. Is it possible that any of the neighborhood women envy her?

a. What about the one whose husband mentioned casually he doesn't like his wife on social media?

   b. What about the woman who joked that she's waiting for retirement, when her family needs her less, to take up a hobby?

9. Do you too, on occasion, wish to leave your hair unattended?
   a. And go without makeup?
   b. Ducking past the women in the courtyard?
   c. Quickly, as though you were hiding something?
   d. Is it possible that hallway smile was one of recognition?

10. Does she recognize something in you?
   a. Your ability to do things alone?
   b. Such as
      i. Raising children?
      ii. And bending the world, a little, to your will?
      iii. A proclivity to magic?

11. Does your power frighten you?
   a. Or, do you find it alluring?
   b. Is it difficult sometimes, because of the ways in which you were socialized, to admit this?

12. Can the odor of a warm broth sometimes be detected, wafting from *your* apartment into hers?
   a. Did you imagine, when you were a girl with two parents and a large family, that you might take such pleasure, once the children were asleep, in cooking for no one in particular?
   b. Do you ever tire of the gaze of others?
   c. If you could pass an entire day, and know that no one would see you, how would you spend it?
   d. Would you step outside as you are, without any fuss or expectations, carelessly, let the wind tousle your messy hair and the sun shine upon your bare face?
   e. You might have to be a witch first, of course. But imagine if you could live as though you were invisible. Imagine if you possessed this power already.
   f. Can you remember for how long you've wanted to learn piano?

g. And dabble with powerful spells?
h. And teach magic to little girls?

Migratory Birds

I'm running in the cold, around a pond lined with tall, amber cattails. A train clatters from beyond the pond. A man calls out my name from behind. I slow, and he jogs up alongside me, tennis shoes hitting the perfectly wide and smooth suburban sidewalks. It's Paul.

I remember something about Paul liking running, saying it cleared his head. I remember Paul sitting on the blacktop at recess, drawing comics, while I sat across from him, reading books.

He says he wasn't sure it was me. I tell him I've gained a little holiday weight, hence the running. He says it wasn't that. He says I run gracefully, and I believe him enough to slow to a fast walk and look at his face full on. Same lidded, dark eyes. Brown, almost black hair. Now, a salt and pepper beard. In the distance, there is a garbled animal croaking. "Like Donald Duck gargling," Paul says.

Izzy wanted to come running, but her grandmother has her involved in a gingerbread project with fresh-baked squares, icing, and gumdrops, the kind of thing I don't make time for but might've in another life. Izzy thrives at my parents' home, my home now, in Houston. She declares even the winter is better than in New York. She keeps the gingerbread home on her nightstand at night to look at, because my mother lets her, and in the morning, they resume decorating. Because it's cloudy outside today, before I left the house, she was stringing marshmallows across the gingerbread roof. "Come back soon, Mom," she said when I left in the morning in my running shoes, and I promised I would. She turned back to her cozy make-believe home, which smells of cinnamon and her grandmother's baking.

When my parents picked Izzy and me up from the airport, on the heels of my separation and the move from New York, Mom wrapped me in a hug. Dad lifted my suitcases and grunted. "Did you fit the whole household in here?" he asked. But I hadn't, not even close. Izzy's dad and I had sold nearly everything, both of us wanting to start fresh. *A house is just a house. Furniture is just furniture*, I repeated to myself until it felt true. Izzy and I sat together in the back seat of Mom's car. "Mom's a kid too," she sang. I worked at a tangle in her brown hair, a copy of mine. I watched her, my spindly seven-year-old in yellow shoes and a bright pink beanie.

"I was hoping to spot an egret," I say to Paul.

A few years ago, a construction company bungled the job of building the sidewalks around the pond that borders my parents' suburb, and took out several trees and a rookery of egrets in nesting season. Their little bodies were everywhere in the morning, the lost parents circling the skies for days, setting off a protest that lasted for weeks. But there are rumors that after years away, the egrets are finally starting to return.

"And you found me instead." He gives a nervous laugh and stops to tie his shoe. "No feathers or beak."

"I'm glad."

He finishes with a double knot. "Me too. I'd look terrible in feathers."

After college, I moved to New York to try my hand at acting but mostly auditioned and worked on the side. One day, I met a director who already had his life figured out and a brownstone in Brooklyn. We began chatting, he mocked my light pink jacket, fresh from Texas, and then we exchanged numbers. By the end of the year, I was living in the brownstone with him.

From time to time, I heard news about Paul back home, first that he'd married the prettiest girl at our school just out of college. And then, later, that she'd gotten restless and left him. Paul and I didn't see each other much after high school, but once, at a local pub when I was visiting home, I went up and introduced myself to him. He'd kicked his boots up against the bar and said, "Of course I remember you, Norah." Then he'd added in an accusing voice, "*You're* the one who left."

Dad was the one who suggested I stay longer for the holiday because Mom's in early-onset Alzheimer's, which I think means Izzy is the one she's most likely to start to forget. But if you can cement the memories now, enough grooves or something on the brain, familiar routes, it's supposed to help a little. None of us are sure quite how it works, but it's quality time. The acting wasn't really going anywhere anyway, and the novelty of being with a clueless Texan had worn off, I suppose, for the director. He was bored of me, it seemed, tired of a life marked mostly by parenting. He and I had been drifting for some time. I agreed to an indefinite holiday, which sealed things between us.

The brownstone is gone now to a new family, the furniture to others. My friend texts, and I slow down to read it, Paul slowing beside me. She asks whether I'll be back in a month to use the tickets she got for us to see a show at the Knitting Factory. She follows up, *We've got a Houston for you in New York too.* I smile but don't answer. I haven't found steady work in either place, so where we'll live is still an open question. I remember Paul has a daughter too, Maria, and I ask about her.

Maria, Paul says, is with her mother across Houston, but he has her half of the time. She's nearly seventeen, a full decade older than Izzy, older than Paul and I were when we met. He asks about Izzy. "And the father?" he says.

I tell him we were never really married, and we're separated now. I confess I'm not sure how it will work with me down here. Maybe Izzy will have to return to New York in the summer. As soon as I say it, I feel the pang. "Maybe I'll go with her, just for summer."

I'm not sure I can even imagine Houston in another season besides this one. I imagine the pond with a permanent winter sky. Since the time I moved away, I've almost never seen it in any season but the space between Christmas and New Year's.

Paul's footsteps beside me are slow and steady, calming even. I tell him I remember the comics he drew at recess, about a superhero flying over the Leaning Tower of Pisa, over the Nile, over the Great Wall of China. Paul says he regrets never going to any of those places, that he's barely left Texas.

"Think I would've done all right in New York like you?" He mulls it over. "I'd be fine. Not sure I would've cared to though."

Another train clatters by. Two little boys walking the trail with a woman in front of us stop to point. The train gives off a ghostly honk, reminding me of the echoing night sounds of my childhood.

I think I remember seeing Paul running around this pond a couple of times after college too. I had a new haircut and an expensive pink running jacket then, which seemed important. I had liked the thought of showing up from New York and running into Paul. This was a time in life, in my twenties, when the thought of impressing someone was more enticing than knowing them. I listened to music through my headphones then and occasionally texted my friends back in New York to tell them how bored I was. I think of that as Paul and I round a turn in the trail.

And then, all at once, we spot them, white feathers against gray. A pair, flying together in distance and coming closer to us, yellow beaks pointing, black legs in downward diagonals, ballet in the sky. "They're back," I murmur. We pause to catch our breaths and watch them sail, skidding to a halt at the edge of the pond.

We stop at the bleachers by the parking lot to stretch our legs and watch the egrets along the shore. Paul asks when I'm heading back home. It takes me a second to figure out whether he's talking about this home or the one in New York.

"I'm not sure about New York," I say. The egrets bob forward along the water's edge, stalking fish, long white necks dipping into the muck. I think about how many seasons I've missed here. I think of Mom and Izzy at home pasting candies on gingerbread. It's the kind of day to sink into doing nothing much at all. Cloudy marshmallows covering the sky.

"I see your parents sometimes," Paul says. "When I'm out that way." I think I regret never telling Paul I liked him.

"They stay close to home these days," I say.

He shrugs. "We gravitate toward the familiar." I lean over to stretch my calves. "Wasn't much of a run," he says.

The sun is rising over the pond, as it always does this time of morning. The water shimmers yellow and white. *Majestic* is the word I will use to describe the egrets and the pond to Izzy and my parents over lunch, as we sample gumdrops, as I tell them about my plans to meet up again with Paul, and Izzy asks us how, after so long away, the egrets ever managed to find their way back home.

The Ballerina

My daughter has a mane, thick as a horse's, and bronze from three weeks ago, when she dyed it. It's impossible to get the whole thing in your hands. Delicate flyaway strands escape my fingers.

She sits on a stool I have wedged in the bathroom. A ray of sun lights up the bronze strands like fire. Truthfully, I prefer her hair loose and free and black, but today, for her recital, I will braid it and wrap it into a bun.

I haven't braided my own hair since I was a dancer. She regards me as though that were a hundred years ago. I pull one section of her hair over, then another. Left and then right, three parts equal.

That's what she wants, three parts—her father, me, and her. But our lives together were an illusion, as weightless as I used to feel when I danced. My feet are heavy now. She will forgive me for having just myself to offer.

We will make a life this way. And it will be just as it was with my mother and me, who had magical fingers that ran through my hair and tugged at my temples. I can feel in my fingertips it will be all right.

When the braid is finished, I wrap it tightly around her head. It will be perfect, and no one will be able to say otherwise. Not the girl at school who called her a show-off, or the boy who said she would look better as a blonde.

When I was a dancer, and the others told me to slim down, I didn't say a word. But my daughter is tougher and fiercer than I was, with eyes of black rock.

I wasn't strong, but I danced as long as I could, even after high school, after my pudge turned into a lump in my belly, after the other girls pointed out I didn't have a ring on my finger, after "fat" was the kindest thing they had called me. It was a small town then too.

The bronze will grow out. Already, I see a sliver of black coming in at the roots.

They will not tell her who she must be. They will not touch her. She will fly away, high, over all of them. I will not hold her down. I will make her understand she never held me down either, not even now, in my heavy black shoes.

I tuck and weave the strands into place, place bobby pins into bronze loops piled upon one another, a basket of hair. I ask her whether she'd like to move away after high school. We think of another town, another life. A slow smile spreads across her face. She says, "What about now?" I imagine the audience waiting, the curtains drawing open, an empty spot on the stage floor, the ballerina's great disappearing act.

Four Little Years

The first time I met Dylan, I was sitting on a rock under a tall oak in the forest behind my house, reading about magic. The mud squelched under his feet as he came over. I didn't look up. I was in the middle of a scene and didn't want to talk. I was also a little stoned because I had, just an hour before, smoked weed with some of my new friends from school. I tried to focus on the page.

"Hello, Sigrid," he said. I nodded back.

It wasn't much of a forest. We lived in a Dallas suburb, next to a field of dairy cows and a tract of land that used to be a brick factory, then a great, long watershed filled with trees and ledges, leading down to a deep creek that rose and fell with the rains.

I liked to get lost in the escarpments behind the house, climbing down to the creek, stalking rabbits, and gathering wildflowers or digging for arrowheads. More often, now that I was getting older, I stopped by the Exxon station at the end of our street to buy Bubble Tape gum and made my way into the forest to sit under a tree and read.

"I thought I was alone. What are you doing here?" Dylan asked. I held up the book.

"Piers Anthony?" he said. "I read him." I nodded once, half surprised he read at all. He was a hick with an odd family, or at least that's how my older brother, Michael, talked about our new neighbors renting the house next door, a boy and a mother, the father off somewhere else, and I'd heard my parents' second-rate excuses (June had homework, Michael had his college applications to go over) for not stopping by when Dylan's mom invited them over.

I reached into my purse, past the Bubble Tape, and pulled out a joint. I'd gotten it from a boy I'd met downtown, who had invited my friend Anna and me to hang out with him and his friends at his apartment. I held it between my fingers and passed it to Dylan. "Know what this is?"

He nodded and took it in one hand. He brought it to his nose and sniffed. I pulled a lighter from my purse, and when he stuck one end in his mouth and leaned forward, I lit it for him. He took a drag, and I held out a hand for my turn.

"Not like that," I said, scolding him the way one of the guys had gently scolded me not two weeks before, my first time smoking a joint. I loved the thrill of it, loved the easy way he pulled it from his mouth and parted his lips a little. I took a drag myself and passed it back to him, a surprisingly intimate motion.

I told him I'd been doing this for years, and didn't know why it came from my mouth that way, but it was so easy that I went with it. It sounded like something the girl I wanted to be would say. Breezy. Confident. I sniffed my fingertips, liking the smell, and looked him over. Dylan was broad shouldered—almost, but not quite, fat. He sat on the edge of a rock now too, hunching forward. He had the body of a football player but lacked the intensity.

And, apparently, he too had read this book about the hapless Bink, who'd been exiled from his homeland for having no magical talent. I was a little embarrassed at having to share the story with him. My solo trips to the woods were my secret. I preferred my friends to think I was at the mall, or at home watching TV. I'd only recently escaped the set of straight-A friends I'd had since elementary school. This year, I sat at lunch with a set who had jobs in retail and on weekends hung out in Deep Ellum to wander through stores, listen to CDs, and smoke weed.

"I love a good escape," he said in his West Texas accent. "This one sneaks up on you. Have you gotten to the big reveal?"

"No spoilers!"

"All right, I won't. I'll just say this. People aren't exactly as they seem. One person—or creature—might easily become another."

It was almost a spoiler, but I didn't get it enough for it to spoil anything. "I'll keep that in mind." I gestured toward the joint. "I'll bet you never tried this back home." He was from a small town, west of Fort Worth.

"Nope, not in Weatherford." He squinted more than smiled. And I wondered if Dylan could feel it too, that feeling of freedom, of almost-release, the feeling I had here in this forest.

"You should come with us to Deep Ellum sometime," I said, feeling generous. "There's much more of that. It's about as far from Weatherford as you can get around here, if that's what you're after."

He shrugged. "Maybe." He took in a deep breath and exhaled. "Whew." He handed the joint back to me and stood up, looking unsteady on his feet. I tucked the joint back into my bag, not wanting to waste what was left.

"Thanks for the gift for June," I said, now remembering. Dylan's mother was a teacher who worked with kids in special education, like my little sister, June. She and Dylan had dropped off some art supplies the week before, extras from her classroom.

Dylan raised a hand to say goodbye, swaying a little on his feet, and I thought about walking back with him but wanted to keep reading, so I said, "Know the way back? Pass the cow pasture and keep going." I felt the weed hit me then too. It was a different feeling from the freedom. Just dizziness and a sense of letting loose, a balloon rising.

Dylan caught his foot in the mud then and slipped, almost falling into the creek. I froze in place. I could've jumped up and caught him, but I didn't move. He righted himself then, getting his hand muddy and then pulling himself up with a branch and wiped the mud on his pants.

"I'm all right," he said. When he said this, I stopped caring whether Dylan had also read the story of Bink and decided it was nice that we shared a book. He had read it at home somewhere in Weatherford, probably hearing it in his head with the little twang, but it was still the same story, about a boy who's no good at anything, who gets exiled from the world of magic and has to find his way.

"All right," I repeated as he plodded back through the muck. I kicked my boot at the puddle at my feet and returned to the page, where my eyes swam pointlessly over the words.

Later, at home, June had her hands folded over one another and was trying to produce a train-whistle sound. She said Dylan had seen her out front and showed her how to do it, except she hadn't been able to get anything but air rushing through her fingers. I couldn't do it myself, so I was no help. I folded my hands and blew, but nothing came.

Michael said he'd driven to the store and seen Dylan hanging over the fence, staring out at the cow pasture for a long time like he was stunned. He asked if he was right in the head, and I told him he was all right, nothing was wrong. Michael wouldn't have cared that I smoked and shared some with Dylan, but I didn't talk to him about it all the same.

"What do you mean, is he all right?" June asked. And then because she had trouble cycling down—that was part of what made her different—she repeated, "What do you *mean*, what do you *mean?*" going up and up. Michael said he was sorry, that he hadn't meant anything, but the whole thing was kind of funny when you thought about it. Such a big guy, hanging on the fence that way, spaced out.

"Who was he looking for?" June asked. "Gino?" Gino was a little calf who'd appeared over the summer, kicking up its feet with a careless joy. We'd spotted him when he was a baby, and what most people didn't know about calves was that calves were just like humans, with little personalities already built in. One could be quiet and sweet, another could be wild. Gino, from what we could gather, was as wild as they came, frolicking, kicking up his little hooves, darting everywhere.

And then, in early September, he'd disappeared from the pasture. We feared something terrible had happened to him. Maybe he'd been sick, or sold, or worse, run into one of those terrible boys who hurt animals for pranks. We didn't know the farmer, so we couldn't ask.

"Yeah, I'll bet he was looking for Gino," Michael said. "Like he was in a trance."

"That's funny," June said. "Moooo."

"Shut up, June," I said. "You're the one obsessed with Gino." It was true. June was only nine but took walks by herself to the pastures to watch the cows. She was the one who'd named the calf.

"Do you know what else Dylan told me?" she said. "Last year, his sister cried so hard when the family went boar hunting, that she actually turned into a boar."

"Shut up," I said. "Nobody turns into anything."

"No, she really did. He said I shouldn't go telling people though, because they wouldn't believe me. And he was right."

Dad, who was passing through the living room, said in a very solemn voice, "June, they do have wild boars in Weatherford, particularly on the outskirts. Who knows? Maybe one of them could be Dylan's sister."

"Don't indulge her, Dad," Michael said.

"Yeah, June," I said with all seriousness. I pushed my finger into her face and said, "You have to face the facts of life."

But our father scooped June up to twirl her around, and she squealed.

My mother called then and said dinner would be ready soon. It smelled like sausage and peppers, something she'd picked up from a French cooking class. All of our friends were jealous of Mom's cooking. She'd said she would have the neighbors over sometime soon for dinner, but I knew she didn't mean Dylan and his mother. And even now, I thought I saw Dylan's mother through the open window, setting the little table for two, putting out plates and utensils properly, though it was just the two of them. And then I thought about poor Gino out there somewhere, missing if he was even alive, and then Dylan.

The next day, at lunch, Sean asked me whether it was true that Dylan was a cowboy, or not a cowboy-cowboy, but obsessed with cows. He'd heard it from my friend Anna, who'd heard it from the seniors. And since I lived next door to Dylan, I ought to know.

I said that it *was* kind of a funny image if it was true, Dylan hanging over the pasture fence and all, his big frame, and Anna laughed and said if we drove by we'd probably see the fence sagging from where he'd leaned against it, and then Sean laughed. I didn't laugh, but no one seemed to notice. There were five of us at our table, all of us sophomores. The rest of them had been friends for years. Of the five of us, I was probably the least funny.

I said it would be funny to get high with Dylan sometime, maybe take him to Deep Ellum with us, and Anna said, "All right, Sigrid, go ask him if you're dying to so much."

"He doesn't want to," Sean said. But I said we wouldn't know unless we asked, and I planned to.

I had a thermos of vodka SlimFast in my lunch and offered Anna a sip. One big thing I had going for me was a constant supply of my parents' wine and liquor, which they never kept locked up, though they rarely drank. I was not like the girls who got shit-faced on weekends, who vomited embarrassingly at parties. I aimed to be worldly and a little aloof, to imbibe without affectation. Just enough to get tipsy, but never so much I couldn't function. At this moment, when I'd ingested the equivalent of two shots, I discovered I could hover around the cafeteria, free of any of them, and see everything: each of us, leaning back easily in our chairs; my old table of friends, carrying on happily without me; Dylan at a table alone, reading a book. The teachers pattering through, chatting with the seniors who would all too soon be gone. All of us, sunk into our respective lives in the most peaceful and boring era of American history to date.

One day, I might just float away from all of them. I thought about this all the time. I would float right away from the same quiet mornings at my house, the clock ticking, my parents absently reading, the same meals, nothing changing. Next year, it would just be June and me at home. Michael was planning to move to New York and not return. I had the sense he was forgetting about me already. He had said to me, "One day, Siggy, you walk in these doors, and the next, you're out of here."

Sometimes, in the school hallway, when I passed by the big pictures of the classes that came before us, in the seventies and the eighties, I looked at their faces and big hair, and I thought, where are you *now*? What's your life like *now*? Do you even remember those four little years of your life? And all I got in return were smiling faces, white teeth, puffy hair and makeup.

I wanted to fit in, but I also knew that all this was temporary. I had senioritis from the moment I got into this school, on account of Michael. That was why I sometimes excused myself from everyone else. Why I disappeared into the forest alone sometimes to think. Why I liked getting high and pretending I was hovering above all of us. There were other dimensions available in this life, and I was interested in all of them. What came next? I didn't know, exactly. But something did, and I was just on the cusp of it.

I was thinking about Dylan now, and his sister, if he even had one at all. I saw him sitting there all alone and tried to imagine why he would tell gullible June some stupid lie about another little girl turning into a boar. Maybe he meant to scare her.

I took a last sip from my thermos and stood up. I went over to Dylan's table, stood there in my oversized green flannel shirt, and said, "Hey. We might go downtown this weekend. Interested? You can come over to the table and meet my friends." I didn't have a crush on him or anything—I just wanted to be nice. He looked past me, not smiling, in the direction of my friends at the table, who were staring his way.

"Can't," he said, mouth turning down derisively. That little twang. "I'll probably be busy."

Dylan kept eating alone at school. I caught him sometimes across the cafeteria, through an arm or elbow, sitting there. He stayed that way through October, and then we were in November, and it was the same thing.

The thing about the cow obsession had stuck. It wasn't a big deal—no one cared much about him, anyway—but it became kind of a joke people threw around, like, *There goes Dylan, off to milk the cows.* Harmless, mostly, though he must have heard it. There was no way he couldn't have.

I didn't join in the teasing but didn't try exactly to stop them either. I'd tried to welcome him. He wasn't interested.

The only one who really talked to him or interacted with him regularly, as far as I could tell, was June. And I hated her a little for going next door like that to spend time with him. Sometimes, I came home and found him in our living room, talking to Mom and June together, like he was taking my place in my family instead of sticking with his own.

One afternoon, when Sean was picking me up to go hang out at Anna's place, he spotted Dylan sitting out on his porch with June, painting canvases at the picnic table.

"It's Farmer Joe," Sean called out to Dylan before he got to my door. I was already on my own porch, waiting to go.

"You're a loser," June called back from next door. Michael and I had schooled her well. We were always sniping at each other.

June had what Mom described as difficulty with tongue and jaw muscle control and could never say words exactly as they were meant to be said. Sometimes I even forgot how different she sounded to others, because it didn't register for me. It was just June.

Sean repeated June's voice just as she sounded, distorting the words. He didn't know June was my sister, since she was on Dylan's porch and they'd never met. But that made it worse.

Dylan got up from the picnic table and moved toward Sean—slow, deliberate, and perfectly clear about what he was going to do. Sean backed away, knocking over a flowerpot in the process. But Dylan came at him, raising his fist back and then forward in a quick, practiced move that flowed all the way through. He hit Sean on one cheek, sending his head to the side and then back in a split moment. Sean doubled over, let out a curse, and I stood there, frozen, taking it in.

I'd thought at one point Sean might've liked me, and even though he supposedly had a girlfriend at another school, I still thought he might. I suspected, in that moment, he might even have been a little jealous of Dylan and how I never teased him. It was hard to say.

"Fuck, man," Sean said, as I stood there, frozen. Then, "Sigrid?" This time, softer. "Siggy?"

I wasn't sure why I didn't stand up for June. Habit, probably. It took a while for things like that to sink in for me. But I hated the look both Dylan and June gave me when I got in Sean's car.

Anna and I gave Sean a cold pack, but he said he didn't need it, the hit wasn't that bad, and besides, it was already cold everywhere. An unusual cold front was sweeping through, threatening snow. In Anna's bedroom, we put on a record, The Velvet Underground. I liked the sixties. I felt as though I were discovering them for the first time, thirty years too late. Sean sat beside me, put a hand on my leg. I guessed I was supposed to feel sorry for him, but instead I got up and moved to the other side of the room. Then Sean and Anna began to move closer together. Anna was birdlike, moved her shoulders in a delicate way to the music, and looped her arm around Sean.

I was sorry the punch hadn't hurt Sean more, and then I realized I was starting to really hate him. We smoked a bowl, and then I lay on Anna's bed, staring at the ceiling, while Sean and Anna shared a kiss, and then their voices hummed around me. Something inside me cracked open then. I thought of June's little face, her puffy cheeks, black eyes, brows furrowed with indignation. Why were she and Dylan so brave, and why wasn't I? I shouldn't have come here. I wasn't sure why I had, except that I had worked so hard and for so long to make them like me.

In this moment, when I found I could hover above us all again, I could see how I really looked. Small, pathetic, alone. In another few years, my face would be on the wall at the high school, then another four years, a hundred years would pass, and if the school was still standing, I would be one of the many ghosts left. What would matter by then? Not Sean. Not Anna. Not this moment.

I said, "I'm going home now." Not *I'd like to.* Just—*I'm going.* And to my surprise, Sean was ready. He grabbed his keys, drove me back, and dropped me off at home.

I knocked on Dylan's door, shivering in the wind. I made sure Sean could see me do it, that I'd chosen to go to Dylan's house instead of mine. When he answered, he shivered in the cold and eyed me suspiciously, the way he looked at the others in school. I told him I had thought about it and was glad he'd punched Sean. That he was the first person ever to stand up for June like that. Then he gave me a shy smile like the one he'd given me in the woods that first day and invited me into the living room. His mother offered me tea, looking hopeful, and then when I declined, she retreated to her bedroom. It was still only 9:30, a half hour before the curfew my parents had set for weeknights.

I wasn't a particularly open person under normal circumstances, but I was too far gone to stop myself from talking. It was a strange thing, finding that capacity that had been hiding in me all this time, and then he opened up too. In the little time we had before my curfew, Dylan told me about Weatherford and his family, about his dad working as a railroad engineer and then getting laid off after a big railroad merger and having to find other work that didn't pay as well. How his mother had gotten this job outside Dallas, and they hadn't figured out where or how to live from here, and whether to keep the house in Weatherford, so each parent had kept one child with them, and it was just meant to be for a little while. How he missed his sister terribly. How she was exactly June's age.

Dylan said he'd liked punching Sean and wasn't sorry for it, though he did ask if Sean was all right. He also wasn't sorry he didn't like it in Dallas, and he didn't want to get used to it or make many friends, because he intended to go home as soon as he could. Except that he liked June, and also, since that day he'd learned that he and I had read the same book, he'd been thinking he might have to give in and like me too.

I think I told him I was sorry, and I believe he said something reassuring. And then we kissed. We were both surprised by it. It was a moment of pure clarity. His lips on mine, an arm tucked around my waist, and him murmuring something I didn't quite catch.

And then it was over. I felt myself turning red as he stared right at me with his green eyes. I panicked. I decided I'd have to pretend at school that nothing had happened between us. I suspected he already understood that.

What I didn't tell him, but meant to, was that I was thinking about being done with that whole set of friends. Instead, I said the one thing that hit me that night, which was that I had decided that no one had to stay anywhere they didn't feel they belonged. That he and I were almost eighteen, and that meant we could get up and go whenever we liked, away from anyone and anything, and that no one could stop us.

Dylan paused for a long beat, and I could see him thinking in the dim light of his living room.

"I'm going to visit my sister," he said.

"The boar?"

He gave a one-sided smile. "I guess I was thinking about that book and shapeshifting when I was talking to June. Anyway, there's tracks that lead straight back. I can do it in three, maybe four days. Just for the holiday. Promise you won't tell anyone till I get there."

"I promise," I said. I had always relished a good secret from the adults. I leaned in for another kiss, but he was staring past me to the windows, to the black night outside.

"I'll take you there sometime, Sigrid, later, if you want to see it. It's not much of a downtown, but you might like it." When he said it, a train outside let out a low whistle, and I felt myself flush with shame over the missed second kiss, and more than that, that I had wanted it so much.

I said I would come see it, with June too, and that satisfied him. He said something about a main street and historic courthouse, but I was getting sleepy and it was my curfew, so I went home.

⁂

It was not long after that, just before Thanksgiving, that Dylan disappeared. He just stopped showing up to classes.

His mother stopped by our house on Thanksgiving afternoon. She was red-faced, with worry lines across her forehead, pushing her hands into her coat pockets, staring across the living room to our table and all the plates set out, telling our mother she was sorry for the disturbance. She asked whether Dylan had been by, and that was when everyone but me learned he was missing.

I didn't know what to say. I had made a promise, and I intended to keep it. At this point June rushed in, saying he was probably off to find his sister, who had turned into a boar. My father said in his solemn way, "June, get on to your room."

Dylan's mother got a funny look and asked, "June, who told you that?" She knew June pretty well from her stopping by all the time to see Dylan and knew she wasn't trying to joke around. June said, "Dylan did." Then June started reaching toward the pumpkin pie we were saving for dessert, but Michael pushed her hand away.

Dylan's mother shook her head and said Dylan's father went boar hunting sometimes, and maybe that was where the story came from. And also that there was nothing wrong with Dylan's sister.

⁂

The next week, Gino came back. I saw him first—standing in the pasture, a little bigger than before, no longer frolicking, now older and more sedate, munching peacefully by the fence. We were sure it was him. Same black-and-white pattern, a dapple of white above his black nose, the same little half-smile. But June said it wasn't Gino, it was Dylan.

"Where did Gino go, then?" Michael teased her. There had been some speculation at school when he didn't show up, and the jokes about Dylan and cows had all stopped. But I kept my mouth shut and waited to hear from him.

"Is there a cow running around somewhere in a boy's body?" Michael asked June. But she didn't answer that. She bounced around the house, flailing her arms, jumping from chair to couch, shrieking, "He's back, he's back," so loud that Mom told her to hush, it wasn't right, the neighbor might hear and get her hopes up. But June didn't stop. She insisted to all of us it was Dylan. How could she tell? She said it was obvious: Dylan's sister had turned into a boar, and he'd chosen a cow.

"You're crazy," I told her. "He's a runaway."

"He's most likely with his dad," Dad said, always logical.

"He turned into what he loved," June said, simple as that.

"If that's true, his little sister must've been in love with boars," I said.

"She must've!" June said, getting into it. "She loved pigs, he loves cows, and I love Dylan!"

"Which form, cow or human?"

"Both!"

"If you love him, maybe you'll turn into him," Michael said.

"Maybe I will," she said, stomping furiously around the house.

If we became what we loved, maybe that's why I felt like I was floating away all the time. Maybe I was disappearing too, swirling up, smoke at the lit end of a joint.

Three Decembers later. I blinked, and all of high school was behind me. Shining new developments. Downed trees everywhere. A yellow digger on the edge of our neighborhood, pulling up the forest, smoothing over the escarpments and piling up dirt to make a park with sidewalks and manicured grass. The Exxon station where I'd bought gum was roped off with yellow tape and soon would become something else.

Already, the house I'd grown up in was one of the older ones. Bright new two-story homes with open windows and floorplans were sprouting everywhere, surrounded by dirt and cleared land. They made our red brick home look small and closed off in comparison. All this time I'd been hoping to escape this place, and instead, it was leaving me behind, a piece at a time.

It was a bright, sunny peacoat day, and I was sitting on the porch with June when Dylan's mother stopped by. I hadn't seen her since she moved away, about a month after Dylan left. I had half believed that every boy I'd kissed since then was about to leave me for good.

"Hello, June," she said, pushing her hands into her coat. "And I thought you might be visiting, Sigrid. I was passing through town and thought I'd see the old house."

June was still using the kinds of paints Dylan and his mother had introduced her to. Our house was full of canvases covered with thick, matted oil paints—outdoor scenes everywhere and, in one, a little dappled black-and-white calf with an unmistakable red smile.

The cow pastures were gone too. The city had bought the land for a new middle school, where June was in the sixth grade now.

I took a drag from my cigarette. I still smoked weed too sometimes but not as often and never around my parents. It had lost its luster by now. It wasn't a magical gateway to anything.

"How are you?" I asked, half afraid to ask. I still thought about how I hadn't shared anything I knew the day Dylan went missing.

"We wanted you to have this." She handed us a stack of paint brushes and blank canvases. June grabbed for them, greedily. We told her about the young couple living in her old house, who hosted parties that sometimes kept June and my parents up at night. I told her I was in college nearby and doing well, and Michael was in New York. I didn't tell her about how sometimes I imagined Michael had turned into a bird, flying away from us all. It was an easier thought than the alternative, which was that he didn't want to visit us.

A train whistled somewhere, like a distant lowing. After Dylan left, June had finally perfected the train whistle with her hands. She did it now, a high whistle echoing the train.

When June went inside to show our parents the paints, Dylan's mother leaned forward and asked in a quiet voice, "Does June know about—"

I shook my head. I didn't know how to explain that June knew Dylan was gone but somehow also thought he'd turned into Gino and then gone on to other pastures. We'd gotten the news at school, of course. Dylan wasn't coming back. The teachers hadn't been able to keep it from us. Our parents saw it in the paper, and then everyone knew. He'd tried to find his way back west but had fallen into a creek and frozen to death halfway between here and Weatherford.

"Oh, Sigrid," she said. I stood up and held my arms open a little, and she moved right into them. Heaving and sobbing, like she'd just been holding it in, all this time, and there it was right under the surface, tears and gulps of air. I held her tight.

And there I was, floating above us all again. Watching myself and Dylan's mother on the little porch in front of the wide sidewalks. The distant train whistled again. It was a haunted sound, an increasingly rare one. It was the sound of tracks, of hauling away, of going away, of disappearing from the whole landscape.

But I didn't float away. I came back to myself. I held Dylan's mom tight and let her shake out all her sobs. The neighbors, Mom and Dad, anybody could think anything they liked about the crying, and my tears that were starting in now too. I didn't know of another way to say I was sorry. I felt her pilled coat under my hands and rubbed her back, round and round until she quieted.

Timetable for Learning to Eat Alone

1 month: The time after which you may wish to dispose of any spices, condiments, or other ingredients the two of you shared. Condiments, though a delight to the taste buds, may, after all, only distract from a deeper need to nourish and satiate. You may begin to try dessert again, a slice of pie perhaps, without your tongue sticking to the roof of your mouth. But it is good to be cautious about the recipe you use. It is too soon for an old one, like your grandmother's pecan pie recipe, which reminds you of the trees that stretched up high arms and littered the yard outside her Fort Worth home with heavy pecans that you scooped up into paper bags and shared with your grandmother as a child. Such recipes are instructions for love, repeated over generations.

2 months: The time it takes for your thumb to fully heal and for you to again, very carefully, curl it under while cutting—a safety technique your mother taught you, which you carelessly disregarded while chopping nuts because your mind was elsewhere, because something felt off.

3 months: You will stop shuddering periodically in front of the gas range while remembering an evening when you were not alone.

4 months: The time it will take for you to use a knife and cutting board without feeling phantom arms around you; also, incidentally, the average number of months couples report it takes to fall in love. Falling out has another timetable entirely.

5 months: You will begin to appreciate your own kitchen enough to cut out a page from a book of poetry, something by David Whyte, with a line that says, *The kettle is singing even as it pours you a drink*, and hang it to the left of your stove. After that, you will fill your window with aloe, thyme, and parsley, and gaze over the pots, outside to the courtyard below, while something simmers behind you, and breathe in a quiet, solitary evening.

6 months: The time it will take you to find the right combination of cinnamon, nutmeg, and clove to approximate the smell of a cozy home. Cinnamon is native to Sri Lanka; ancient Egyptians used it in embalming, and the Roman Emperor Nero is said to have ordered a year's supply to be burned after he murdered his wife. In the seventeenth and eighteenth centuries, various European countries fought each other over access to these spices. In modern times, particularly in winter, the warm scent may be used as a substitute for the elusive feeling of romantic and familial love.

7 months: You can sip green tea without feeling a tingle down your spine, the way you felt when he slipped outside for phone calls while you heated the kettle. The phone calls usually went on quietly, with him smoking a cigarette, pacing, and once, when you were taking out the trash, you thought you caught the particular pitch of a woman's voice on the other end.

8 months: The time it takes to drive by the house you moved into together, complete with the renovated kitchen and gas burners, without feeling your stomach drop. Incidentally, the layout reminded you of one particular summer dinner from your childhood: your mother spooning out a chicken and rice dish, your father pouring honey onto white dinner rolls, and the gentle rolling of your contented stomach as you savored the last bites.

9 months: You can experience the quiet satisfaction of a vegetarian noodle recipe you've chosen, with ripe squash and tomatoes that give just so—a meal made with care by one and for one only. This meal will far surpass any of the others, and years later, you will remember with wonder the aroma, the sizzling skillet, the skillful cuts made by your own hands.

10 months: The time it will take you to finally pull out the wooden tray you had carefully arranged with cheeses and other treats for your guests the night you happened to come upon him kissing another woman in the kitchen next to a pie cooling on the gas stovetop. The same night the knife slipped while you were chopping nuts, and he bandaged your thumb gently with cheesecloth. You could not help but hear the tenor of the other voice and find it similar to the one you thought might have been coming through the receiver in those quiet evening calls.

11 months: The time it will take to make another pecan pie like the one you made before the guests arrived, when he wrapped his arms around you and said, "Careful, you're going to make me marry you." It would not be the memory of the pie, much later, that would make you shudder in front of the gas range, but the other part. Food, after all, is transitory, passing through your digestive system, except, of course, for those portions that remain with you and become part of the fabric of your cells. Recipes only gain significance when served with true affection.

12 months: The time it takes for a cheese tray or a knife to lose any special meaning. After all, they are merely utensils. This is the time it takes, more or less, for an old pie spatula to settle in the back of a drawer and become nothing more than a metal triangle attached to a black wooden cylinder, a tool for slicing through a gooey mess that itself is nothing more than a sweet, empty concoction.

This Is Happiness

Ed and I are staying at a Virginia farmhouse with a chicken coop out back and a proprietor who serves red wine before dinner and complains about the neighbor's goats getting into her blueberry bushes. There is only one other couple at dinner, a slender woman with a black and gray bun knotted at her neck and a man with deep frown lines and a beard, both musicians from the National Symphony Orchestra.

Ed is explaining to everyone at dinner that life satisfaction follows a basic U shape, a figure he traces with his finger through the air, down to the table and back up again. I'm following his eyes and waiting for them to meet mine, for the kind of surreptitious half-smile he'd give across the table when we first met. He continues gesturing toward the couple and says the dip is supposed to come sometime in late middle age before it starts rising again. But all I can see are the two dots he punctuates precisely on either side of the dip with his index finger, dots of happiness.

The woman is a violinist. We don't know what the man plays because he only goes on about her, while she ducks her head to one side and smiles. They've been seeing each other only a few months, they say, and although we're younger, we're more experienced in the business of our love, a few years past the honeymoon and a bit into the work of it. When Ed's eyes finally meet mine, I recognize his look, which is saying this is the couple we overheard the previous night, laughing through the walls, shaking the headboard of the bed while we brushed our teeth and rolled our eyes.

The woman tells us, as we wait for the main course, that she's been in Washington, DC, where they live now, for the briefest time. He's lived in the city most of his life, and they wouldn't have met at all, except that she won the orchestra position earlier this year and moved there.

It was only a matter of chance, she says, that one of the violinists developed arthritis and stopped playing, leaving a symphony spot open, which she auditioned for and won. The woman says she waited decades to join a full symphony, taught private lessons most of her life, and had almost given up hope. She gives a great shrug, and she and the man laugh together, as if baffled by the idea of so much joy. As they do, Ed's hand finds its way to my knee.

Just then, as the late sun stretches onto the white tablecloth, my wine glass slips from my hand, and I spill the Cabernet. The red seeps into the tablecloth, watery and pink, and the delicate glass rolls off and clatters to the floor. The woman who owns the place tells me it's no worry, not about the cracked glass either, which has splintered off in the floorspace around my sandals.

I dab at my shirt as dinner arrives. When Ed grabs my hand under the table, I notice him watching the violinist gaze at her lover as she takes her first bite of the Brunswick stew.

After dinner, the other couple invites us on their nightly walk. We go out through French doors to see the land behind the farmhouse, beneath the violet outline of the Blue Ridge Mountains, into a landscape that has nothing to do with our life back home. As we watch a greedy goat stretching its neck under a fence to nibble berries, the man grabs a blue flower for the violinist from a bush and tucks it behind her ear. When the sky turns pink, Ed finds two perfect halves of a robin egg in the pathway, picks them up, and holds one-half out to me. The outside is a soft blue, the color of Easter eggs.

If you look closely, he tells me, there is the tiniest whorl of deeper blue inside the lighter blue of the shell's surface. He holds his half up to the setting sun to show me and then sets it on the pad of my finger. The goat sticks its neck further through the fence, just missing the last of the berries he's reaching for, while the chickens cluck.

Or was the chicken coop out front? And was June too early for the blueberries? And at what point did the violinist retrieve her instrument for the evening performance, while her lover looked on? I will try to piece it together in the fall, after Ed and I have stopped sharing meals again, and I ask him if he wants to go to the orchestra like we said we would, or perhaps another B&B in the Virginia countryside would do it. I'll remember the violin that was playing, and the case propped open with its velvet blue insides, the way the man watched as the violinist drew her long bow backward, chin resting, face upward, and filling the summer sky with the sound of vibrations. And of course, the egg.

In one second, before I can get close enough to see the whorl of color, the wind whips the robin blue eggshell off my finger. The sun sits behind the mountains, and floating on the breeze, somewhere above us, the eggshell defies gravity, mixing with the soft vibrato of a violin, slow lows and highs building up toward a single moment. Isn't it funny, all that work of the rising up, all the falling to be done, just for one tiny moment on an upside-down U, as the violin hits a clear note and the eggshell hovers at the top of a perfect arc.

Randomized Trial

The fourth-grade student council gathered round in a semicircle of wooden desks. Brady raised his hand and said, "It seems like Ivy isn't pulling her weight around here. I hate to be the one to say it, but somebody's got to."

There was an uncomfortable set of nods around the table. "She hasn't learned any of her multiplication tables," Lars said. "She demonstrates a willingness to learn, but perhaps," he lowered his voice, "not a *capacity.*"

There was talk of recommending Ivy for a performance improvement plan—the dreaded *PIP*, with a lecture from Ms. Stevenson, the student council sponsor, complete with check-ins, performance measurements, and an equally dire requirement to write SMART goals (*specific, measurable, achievable...*) for herself. In the meantime, Ivy's privileges and bonus would be restricted: one Now and Later candy instead of the standard three before long weekends, and a slice of recess cut off to create time for an independent study on the benefits of a learning mindset.

Over the next few days, Ivy was docked several points at recess for using blades of grass to make duck calls, attempting to make the train-whistle sound with her hands, and wishing too many times upon wish flowers. She was asked to write a three-paragraph essay about how each of those activities might contribute toward a college application and could not think of a suitable answer. The wishes were proven to be ridiculous: a pony to ride upon (not feasible within city limits), a slide from her bunk bed to the garden outside (way outside her parents' budget), and to be able to understand her cat's *meows* (displaying a remarkably poor comprehension of science). And upon close inspection, Ivy's SMART goals were actually types of candy she was craving, which caused Brady to remark under his breath, "Parents should've named her something else. She's never getting into one of those."

Ivy did have one remarkable talent though, which even Brady had to acknowledge, and it was this: headstands. Headstands were not formally on the curriculum, nor was there a rubric for them, but Ivy's headstands were impressive. While other students struggled to balance even on one leg, Ivy could stand on her head for upward of ten minutes.

"How does the blood not rush to her head?" they wondered aloud in Ivy's performance check-in. "What does she think about all the time that she's like that? Couldn't she be using that time to study?" And, they asked themselves, "Are the headstands contributing or detracting from her learning?"

"Maybe," Lars said, "the headstands are what's stunting her learning."

And so the student council, in its quest for evidence-based solutions to educational performance, decided upon a test to figure out whether Ivy should be allowed to continue balancing upside down. Brady was the first to try it. He leaned against a wall, balanced on his head, and kicked his feet up above him. Then came Lars, Gina, Devon, Rebecca, and Aurora, the blood rushing to their heads, feeling the funny, dizzying feeling in their stomachs and the little pings of joy as they kicked ever so slightly off the walls. (Joseph, the seventh council member, was missing due to a scheduling conflict with an SAT prep course.)

Brady felt it first. "Distracting," he murmured. He didn't know how to continue the sentence or whether he should. "Not terribly productive, but—"

"It's rather—" Lars started but couldn't continue either. *Fun* was an embarrassing word. "Pleasingly effective."

Gina said it was possible the position could help one to see situations in new ways, a bit like changing the font of a Word document.

Devon said the whole thing made him a little sick, but it might also have been the sushi and carrot sticks he'd had for lunch.

Rebecca said that for someone who was already behind grade level, the headstand might have an impact, though it would be impossible for someone with her scores to know.

Aurora said she had seen *everything* now, and wouldn't it be funny if Ms. Stevenson walked in right now and saw all of them like this, and that they'd better write up a report to document their findings.

But the report stalled, because the student council couldn't agree on what its parameters should be, including *what* exactly they were measuring, or by what indicators they could determine Ivy's suitability for headstands.

They decided it would be prudent for Ivy to limit her headstands, in the meantime, to the main classroom during student council meetings, so she could be observed. And so Ivy moved indoors during recess and began doing her headstands in the classroom, while the student council watched.

It was observed that Ivy sometimes sang under her breath during her headstands.

There were multiple accounts of her smiling suspiciously to herself.

At various points, Ivy bicycled her feet instead of remaining perfectly still, possibly to improve her balance. On one occasion of vigorous bicycling, one of her Crocs flew across the room.

When at last the council members were about to give up on ever having an explanation for Ivy's conduct, or a measurement of its effects, Gina decided to observe Ivy while also upside down herself. She explained, "It might be the only way to understand her from a new angle."

Aurora, who was also the secretary for monitoring and evaluation, said it was important to replicate results across studies, and so she too joined Gina in a headstand alongside Ivy.

Rebecca first said she would never, but then changed her mind after Aurora joined.

Only Devon, Lars, and Brady stayed upright, insisting that participating in the experiment would taint the results. This conclusion naturally led to murmurs among the upside-down girls and a standoff within the student council, which, until now had always operated with unanimity.

Rebecca noted, at this point, that Ms. Stevenson had recently been spending the entire student council period in the teachers' lounge. She wondered aloud whether they could even count on Ms. Stevenson to settle things, if it came down to it.

"If it came down to *what*?" Brady asked.

"If the experiment fails?" Gina suggested.

"If the council isn't up to the task," Rebecca said.

"Of course we're up to it," Lars said.

Two of the upside-down girls exchanged a smirk. Rebecca gave a small patronizing laugh. "It must feel nice to think so," she said.

At that, Brady gave Rebecca's foot a shove, tipping her sideways onto the floor. Rebecca, misjudging the shoes she'd seen coming toward her, and thinking it was Lars who'd done it, pushed Lars into a whiteboard, knocking down a shelf of dry-erase markers. Gina, who had always liked Lars, shoved Rebecca. Aurora, who'd been jealous of Gina ever since she'd won the spelling bee in third grade, took the opportunity to kick her in the shins.

It was just then that the seventh council member, Joseph, arrived. (He had decided to pause his SAT prep until he could be sure the test's format wouldn't change again.) He opened the classroom door to find a scrum of fourth graders kicking and pushing, shoving and pulling hair, and in the center of the room, one little upside-down blonde girl, bicycling her legs as fast as they would go. Joseph did the only thing there was to do: he made a note of it in the minutes.

The official assessment was unanimous: Ivy's headstands should not be allowed to continue. But due to a point of procedure, the council's decision was unenforceable. At the time of the report's delivery, the chief enforcement officer, Ms. Stevenson, was in the teachers' lounge, unfurling a small plastic wrapper from a Now and Later and savoring its flavor while devouring a romance novel. She mistook the report for yet another bulletin on improving student test scores and tossed it promptly into the recycling bin.

Without an enforcement mechanism, Ivy was allowed, and even encouraged, in her quirks. By springtime, her test scores had improved the most dramatically of any fourth grader's. But when no one could say whether it was due to correlation or causation, the fourth-grade parents' listserv exploded, demanding answers. The parents found it inconceivable that one child should be allowed to excel so dramatically, without the school replicating the results for the others. Several of the parents called the school board for answers. One threatened, in a message through the parent-teacher app, to have the teachers fired. Ms. Stevenson resigned, and the student council was disbanded. Under the principal's direction, upside-down strengthening positions were formally added to the curriculum, with a rubric for testing posture, time in position, and the appropriate attributes to display while exercising. Ivy was named as an interim teachers' aid for monitoring and evaluation. But by the end of her first day on the job, Ivy had abandoned the idea of headstands. The teachers were left to puzzle through her notes in the comments section of the rubrics she was filling out on her classmates—doodles of ponies prancing through the sky, kitties with top hats, the words in a thought bubble above one of the kitties: *I quit.*

Acknowledgments

Grateful acknowledgment is made to the publications in which these stories first appeared, in slightly different forms and (in some cases) under slightly different titles.

"The Shape-Shifter" appeared in *Atticus Review*
"Domestication" appeared in *Flyway*
"Proportions" appeared in *Pithead Chapel*
"Before All That" appeared in *Heavy Feather Review*
"Regression" appeared in *Funicular Magazine*
"Clementine" appeared in *The Antioch Review*
"Skin Like Snake" appeared in *The Offing*
"Nine Hundred Miles to Tampa" appeared in *Cutleaf*
"Plastic Teeth" appeared in *Fiction Southeast*
"Room for Three" appeared in *Red Rock Review*
"Dinnertime" appeared in *Roanoke Review*
"Dreams of a Sleek, Gray Sofa with Tufted Cushions" appeared in *LEON Literary Review*
"Manna" appeared in *Relief: A Journal of Art and Faith*
"Ain't Gonna Stick" appeared in *100 Word Story*
"The Inner Chamber" appeared in *Popshot Quarterly*
"Brown-Eyed Recluse" appeared in *The Maine Review*
"The Long Brew" appeared in *Literary Mama*
"In the Great Grown-Up Game of Make-Believe" appeared in *(mac)ro(mic)*
"It Wasn't a Fit" appeared in *jmww*
"Evening by the Lake" appeared in *Southern Humanities Review*

"Is She a Witch? A Quiz" appeared in *Maudlin House*
"The Ballerina" appeared in *Lunch Ticket*
"Timetable for Learning to Eat Alone" appeared in *Moon City Review* and *Best Small Fictions 2024*
"This Is Happiness" appeared in *Gordon Square Review*

I am grateful to that first little writing group I had in New York City, from 2005 to 2007. Nancy, Marisa, Beth: Thank you for those lovely after-hours coffees and drinks in Midtown and the first sharing of pages that convinced me I could try this thing called fiction. Thank you to the big steps of the post office on Eighth Avenue, which I would trudge up during my lunch breaks from the nonprofit where I worked, feeling a little grand, sending off my first stories. (None of them were accepted, but one received a kind rejection that was one of my first great joys in writing.)

I'm grateful to the writers' groups born out of the classes I took at The Writer's Center (Ginny, Cathy, Deb, Michael, Frank, and many others) and to the groups after that, including the Literary Liaisons group (for eleven years! Norah, Rita, Jim, Allie, and before that, Kenny, Tom, and others). Also to Kristi, Emily, Anna, Mandy, Allison, Prerna, and Abi for your writing feedback. And to friends who have supported me through it all: Karen, Annie, Charlene, and other dear friends I've made and held through DC's writing community.

The DC Commission on the Arts and Humanities generously supported my work through their grant programs. Autumn House Press has been really wonderful to work with. Thank you, Kristen Arnett, for judging and selecting this collection. Thank you, Christine, for all you do for Autumn House authors. And thank you, Hattie, for your patience, your keen editorial eye, and sense of story in working with me to sharpen this collection. I'm grateful to Kinsley Stocum for producing a beautiful cover.

Finally, my thanks go to my family: to my parents for believing in me with a light touch and without pressure, and to my sister and brother and their partners for being loving presences in our lives. I'm grateful to my kids for their love and support. It's not always easy to have a mother who disappears to write or to attend writing groups that disrupt bedtime routines. Thank you to Genevieve and Benjamin, who have brought me joy from your births, and to Sadie and Julian, whom I've been lucky to know for nearly five years. You've all brought so much richness and a lot of laughs. And thanks, finally, to my husband, Andrew, who has been a wonderful partner to have in life through all of it.

New & Forthcoming From Autumn House Press

Bigger: Essays by Ren Cedar Fuller
Winner of the 2024 Nonfiction Prize, selected by Clifford Thompson

self-driving by Betsy Fagin
Winner of the 2024 Poetry Prize, selected by Kazim Ali

Interlocutor Goddess by Jasmine Reid
Winner of the 2024 CAAPP Book Prize, selected by Aracelis Girmay

Self Portrait as the "i" in Florida by P. Scott Cunningham
Winner of the 2025 Donald Justice Poetry Prize, selected by Major Jackson

Les Portes by Meredith Nnoka
Winner of the 2025 CAAPP Book Prize, selected by Cameron Awkward-Rich

Magdalena Is Brighter Than You Think by Grace Spulak
Winner of the 2025 Rising Writer Prize, selected by K-Ming Chang

Winners of the Autumn House Press Fiction Prize

Near Strangers **by Marian Crotty,** selected by Pam Houston

The Neorealist in Winter: Stories **by Salvatore Pane,** selected by Venita Blackburn

Entry Level **by Wendy Wimmer,** selected by Deesha Philyaw

Molly **by Kevin Honold,** selected by Dan Chaon

Further News of Defeat: Stories **by Michael X. Wang,** selected by Aimee Bender

Not Dead Yet and Other Stories **by Hadley Moore,** selected by Dana Johnson

Carry You **by Glori Simmons,** selected by Amina Gautier

Heavy Metal **by Andrew Bourelle,** selected by William Lychack

Bull and Other Stories **by Kathy Anderson,** selected by Sharon Dilworth

Truth Poker **by Mark Brazaitis,** selected by Sharon Dilworth

Come By Here **by Tom Noyes,** selected by Kathleen George

What You Are Now Enjoying **by Sarah Gerkensmeyer,** selected by Stewart O'Nan

Favorite Monster **by Sharma Shields,** selected by Stewart O'Nan

Peter Never Came **by Ashley Cowger,** selected by Sharon Dilworth

Attention Please Now **by Matthew Pitt,** selected by Sharon Dilworth

Drift and Swerve **by Samuel Ligon,** selected by Sharon Dilworth